ON THE RUN

Behind Frazer and gaining with every stumbling stride of his dead-tired stallion were the bully boy riders of the Big T spread. Frazer could hear the reports of their Colt .45s and Winchesters, feel the whizz of bullets coming closer.

In front of Frazer was a raging river without a bridge; there was no hope of swimming it.

Death by shooting or death by drowning—a hard choice for a man.

But Frazer wasn't thinking of dying. What he had in mind was killing. . . .

Charles N. Heckelmann
FIGHTING RAMROD

POPULAR LIBRARY • NEW YORK

Published by Popular Library, CBS Publications,
CBS Consumer Publishing, a Division of CBS Inc., by
arrangement with the author

September, 1977

Copyright 1951 by Charles N. Heckelmann

ISBN: 0-445-04058-0

To Lorraine and Tommy

1   Long Jack McKelvey's deep voice rumbled to a halt as he slowly closed the battered Bible from which he had read the marriage service. It was all over now. Ella Land and Van Winston were husband and wife.

There was a sudden stir among the men and women crowded into the Circle W ranch's big living room. Chairs scraped along the floor as people surged to their feet. Voices which had been respectfully stilled during the brief ceremony now rose in a sibilant murmur.

McKelvey, the only parson in Two Forks, smiled down at Ella Land—now Ella Winston—from his great, gangling height. She turned away, not smiling at all. She felt Van Winston's insistent tug on her arm. Then his big, clumsily eager hands pulled her against his chest. His mouth descended quickly, avidly, toward her face. His lips imprisoned hers, sucking them close and holding on.

The guests were moving forward. Chairs were pushed aside. Ella gathered her strength. With a convulsive jerk she shoved Winston away.

"What's the matter?" he said. The words were thick and the frown that was never far away from his dark brows rushed like a black shadow across his features.

"I like to be kissed—but not like a man would kiss a

5

honky-tonk girl," she murmured. Again there was no smile on her proud, sultry face.

"Just what do you mean by that?" he asked.

Ella stood straight and stiff before him. Color rode her firmly molded cheeks. Her answer held a taut biting quality. "I don't like rough handling—even from a husband."

Always quick to take affront, Winston stepped toward Ella. His hand reached for her and his eyes were like tiny marbles—black and hard as agate. Then the guests surged around them. If they had heard the sharp exchange between bride and groom none gave any sign.

In a moment Ella and Van were separated. Women and girls clustered around Ella, talking and laughing. Bess Landon, wife of Sheriff Fred Landon, reached Ella first. She kissed her warmly. "Good luck, Ella."

Ella smiled faintly. It was a tired, cynical gesture. "Thanks," she said. Automatically she held out her hand to the next woman in line, Mrs. Dale Roush.

Bess Landon moved on, shooting a swift side glance toward Van Winston. He stood a few feet away, talking to two men. One was Ben Revere, owner of the Two Forks bank. The other was Odd Kirkman, proprietor of the Mercantile. The townsmen were congratulating Winston and pumping his hand. But Winston wasn't paying much attention. He kept watching Ella with a morose and brooding interest. At the moment he appeared to be anything but a bridegroom.

Oddly enough, of the twenty or so ranchers and cowpunchers who had been in the room, most of them had not come forward to extend their good wishes to Winston. Even as the Circle W owner's glance shifted to the end of the room four more range-clad men pushed through the open doorway and out onto the veranda. The few who did wander forward to shake hands with Winston did so hur-

6

riedly, as if it were an unpleasant task that had to be seen through merely for the sake of propriety.

Ella was still surrounded by women. But as with Winston, there was a distinct air of unease in the way the ranch wives and younger girls greeted her. They, too, seemed to be in a hurry. They lingered for a brief touch of hands, a perfunctory kiss, then pushed their way through the scattered profusion of chairs to the veranda doorway.

The dark, almost smoldering quality in Ella's green eyes deepened. The slight hollows below her cheekbones became more pronounced. With her raven-black hair, thin curving brows, and finely sculptured face she was beautiful. But it was a cold sort of beauty. Her wedding gown was a long gray taffeta dress with a tight bodice that showed off the full, mature swell of her bosom. It lent additional height to her slender figure already inches taller than that of her husband.

As the room gradually cleared of people Ella stared over the heads of those nearest to her. She searched the shadowy area near the far doorway. Her manner plainly showed that she was looking for someone. For a brief moment, as her eyes settled on a figure lounging against the wall, she seemed to brighten. Winston, too, saw the man who had caught Ella's attention. Immediately his heavy lips clamped tight.

Several chaps-clad punchers wearing fresh shirts and bandannas, their boots highly polished for the occasion, moved en masse toward Ella. But the tall, broad-shouldered figure by the door did not stir. A stream of smoke dribbled past the man's lips as he took a drag at a cigarette. Quietly he peered over the screen of smoke at Ella and Winston.

Then Ella forgot the figure at the door as Margo Nash from the Double-Y outfit came up and took her hand.

7

"My best wishes, Ella," Margo said.

She was a hardy, range-bred girl. At twenty-two she was in the full bloom of womanhood. Her tall, straight body was generously curved and proportioned and she walked with a lithe, easy grace. Bright, long-lashed gray eyes and a wide, red-lipped mouth gave a ruddy glow of vitality and health to her features.

Ella's thin mouth quirked. "Sure you mean that?" she asked.

"Why not?" said Margo. The sultry look she knew so well was a banner in Ella's eyes. Both girls were the same age. Yet there was an odd brittleness in Ella's manner, a certain barrenness of spirit that made her appear older. Margo, thinking of many things that were done and gone now, said softly: "You've got your man."

Ella's lips hardly moved. "Have I?"

Margo looked at her again and was saddened. What most of the range had long suspected she knew to be true. This had been a marriage of convenience. Winston was ten years older than Ella, set in his ways, dour and unfriendly, and cordially disliked by most of the other cowmen in Two Forks. But he had money and influence—things Ella had never had and always wanted.

Well, she had them. And already she was sorry. The dead gray hue of her skin, the taut down-curve of her mouth told Margo all she needed to know. And with it came a twinge of something else—a nagging finger of worry that concerned her.

She turned away from Ella. She couldn't trust herself to speak. Harry Yorke, one of her own punchers moving up to congratulate Ella, called a greeting but she did not hear him. She circled a huddle of chairs, angling for the doorway and the lone man smoking a cigarette there. A wary tightness was in her cheeks.

Somehow she managed a smile when Tom Frazer, ram-

8

rod of the Double-Y ranch which she had been running for the past year while her father was recuperating from a serious illness out in Frisco, pushed his long, muscular body away from the wall and swung down the room toward Ella.

He waved to Margo, not saying anything. She walked on. But something deep and compelling inside her drew her to a halt at the edge of the veranda. She told herself she wouldn't look back. But she did.

She saw Harry Yorke, Tex White, and Hal Cooper, all from her own ranch, pause briefly to shake Ella's hand, then moved on. She saw Winston start toward Ella, then turn irritably as Mrs. Landon caught him by the arm and filled the air with her idle talk. And she saw Tom Frazer bend down and kiss Ella full on the lips. It was something none of the other men had dared to do in front of Winston.

Margo closed her eyes, not wanting to see any more. She went out across the veranda and into the sunlight of the front yard.

Frazer's kiss was brief and impersonal. Yet even the short contact with Ella's lips stirred the embers of an old fire in him. There had been a time when he had once thought of himself in Winston's place. Ella could get down inside a man and shake him up. He knew. But she wasn't any good for him. Nor for any man.

"Well, aren't you going to say something?" Ella's voice held a note of mockery.

"You've gone and done it," Frazer said. "I wish you the best."

"Thanks," she said. "I'll probably need it." An odd fatalism colored her talk. Then her manner altered. Her next words whipped at him with razor keenness. "Where's Bill? I've got to see him."

9

Frazer's wide-spaced blue eyes clouded up. "That's all over. Forget him."

"No, you're wrong," Ella said with swift passion. "It'll never be over."

"Keep off," Frazer warned. "You're only buying trouble."

"Maybe I like trouble."

Frazer was about to reply when he saw out of a corner of his eye that Van Winston had finally rid himself of Mrs. Landon and was striding toward them. Frazer gave Ella a warning look, then wheeled to face Winston.

"Congratulations," said Frazer.

Winston nodded surlily. He stared at Frazer's outstretched hand but made no move to take it. Antagonism, solid as a physical blow, rolled out from the Circle W rancher. Winston had the big rancher's intolerance for small cowmen and for hired hands. He treated his own crew with little consideration. He had stepped on a number of people to reach his present level of prosperity. He would step on a lot more before his days were done.

Yet, watching him with a strict attention, Frazer knew that a gnawing jealousy was at the root of Winston's hostility. Winston was aware that Ella and Frazer had once been very close. Because he was a thorough realist he understood how cold and calculated an affair his marriage was. He owned Ella in name. But how much of her did he really have? This was the question tormenting the rancher's mind. Winston was eating his heart out. Every kiss Ella had ever given to another man would be just so much more stored-up pain for Winston, whose appetite for possession amounted almost to a mania. There was fear in him—fear that Ella had not stopped loving Frazer, had not stopped wanting him.

It was this fear that prompted Winston's savagery.

"You've had your kiss, Frazer," he said. "You understand it's the last."

Temper flared hotly in Frazer's blue eyes. The muscles strung across his wide, deep chest quivered with sudden tension. His arms stiffened. His hands knotted into hard balls. He wasn't a redhead for nothing. Violence was never far from the surface of his emotions. He had had his share of rough-and-tumble scraps. Action was the core of his being. A lump on the bridge of his nose was nothing but a relic of a past fight and a break in the cartilage that had never been repaired. He had smoothly planed cheeks, tanned a deep brown by the sun. His mouth was straight and firm, hinting at the bulldog tenacity that was so much a part of his nature.

Now he took a hitch in his black trousers, shifted the heavy cartridge belt around his waist, and let the full weight of his aroused glance settle on Winston. He was completely aware of what Winston was driving at. But the streak of mule-headedness that went with his red hair impelled him to strike back. "If you've got something on your mind, better get it off now, Winston."

Ella leaped into the breach. "This is no time for you two to be fighting," she said. She took Winston's arm. "They'll be putting the food on the tables outside. Come on. I'm hungry."

Winston glowered at Frazer but let himself be led toward the door. Frazer followed a few feet behind, his spurs jangling with every step. Somehow the sound was a discordant bell in his mind. It filled him with a vague sense of uneasiness. He watched the retreating shapes of Ella and Winston and saw only trouble ahead—trouble for Ella and for anyone else she permitted herself to be friendly with.

Outside in the front yard Frazer saw that heavy planks had been set up on sawhorses to form two huge tables.

11

Two benches from the bunkhouse had been dragged out along with some wooden crates to serve as extra chairs. The tables had been rigged up under some cottonwoods.

Already some of the older women were pitching in to help Mrs. Belle Loring, Winston's widowed housekeeper, bring out the food which had been under preparation in the cook shack. The sheriff's portly, talkative wife appeared with a platter of fried steaks. Another woman followed with two bowls of steaming potatoes. There were heaping dishes of baked beans, other bowls of tinned tomatoes, and great mugs of coffee.

Rigs and buckboards and saddle horses were tethered in various places around the yard. A crude rope corral had been formed between four trees a short distance from the barn. Into that enclosure a number of horses had been hazed and a Circle W puncher was keeping an eye on them.

There was a small keg of whisky under the trees for the men. Another Circle W puncher was in charge. He saw that the tin cups were filled. There wasn't much talk or laughter despite the drinking. Nor was there any mingling of the various ranch crews. The three Double-Y waddies who had come to the wedding with Margo and Frazer kept to themselves or mingled briefly with the punchers from Dale Roush's or Ad Simmons's place.

Mrs. Loring lifted her voice to a shout, calling the men over to the tables to eat. Slowly, in twos and threes, they wandered across the yard and sat down. Frazer spotted Bill Corey near the whisky keg and moved toward him. Corey saw him coming, drained the liquor from his cup, and flung it away. Then he walked over. Before he reached Frazer he paused to fling up a hand at Ella, who looked toward him as she sat down beside Winston at one of the tables.

12

"Ella was asking for you," Frazer told Corey. "Aren't you going to wish her luck on her wedding day?"

Corey's long mouth twisted in a cynical smile. "Sure, Tom. I've got lots of time."

Corey was a heavy-thewed man. He had a ruddy complexion, dark blue eyes, and a mercurial temperament. His sun-browned features were marked by a handsome irregularity; the cheekbones were high and prominent, the mouth full and a little sensuous. He had a mocking, devil-may-care air about him. Yet there were times when his mood changed. At these times he was apt to be surly and truculent. There was almost a vicious restlessness about him. He had no solidity, no real roots.

"Time's run out for you now," Frazer told him.

Corey shrugged and said softly: "I thought you knew Ella better than that."

"That's what I'm worried about."

Corey threw an arm about Frazer's shoulder. They were of equal height. Corey was broader and heavier. But there was just as much spring-steel strength in Frazer.

"Kid, don't worry," Corey murmured. "You'll be old before your time. Life is too short."

They moved off together to the end bench at one of the tables. Frazer couldn't shake off a feeling of depression. Corey's answer was typical of the man. He was a rash, unthinking individual. The two friends had done their share of helling around together. Though they were opposites in temperament they had always hit it off well. Frazer, despite his own recklessness, acted as a checkrein on Corey, curbing the latter's tendency toward wild excesses.

Lately Frazer had concerned himself with the way in which Corey was letting his one-man cow spread run down. Corey had developed a streak of lazy carelessness which was alarming. He avoided routine ranch work. He

13

spent more and more time in town gambling and drinking.

Frazer ate mechanically, hardly tasting the food that was heaped on his plate by one of the rancher's wives. He kept thinking of Corey. Once or twice he saw Corey exchange a surreptitious glance with Ella. Each time he saw color heighten the girl's cheeks. He saw, too, how Winston, feeling the couple of long slugs of liquor he had sampled, had tried to embrace Ella at the head of the table. There had been a brief struggle. Winston had taken his kiss. But Ella hadn't been gracious about it and resentment was building up inside Winston. It showed in the grim, silent way he attacked his food.

Suddenly the meal was over. People began drifting away from the tables. Dale Roush engaged Frazer in conversation for a moment. Then Winston called for Mrs. Loring to clear away the food and plates, adding pointedly that his neighbors had work to do just as he did and would want to be on their way.

It was a blunt and tactless thing to say. At any other ranch a wedding party such as this would have lasted all afternoon and well into the night. But Winston was not a genial host. He resented the intrusion of ranchers who, if it had not been for the wedding, would never have come near the Circle W spread. Immediately there was a general rush toward rigs and horses.

Frazer looked around for Corey but did not see him. Ella, too, was missing. Winston was talking in low tones to his housekeeper. Frazer saw the woman shake her head in reply to a question. Then Winston scowled and trudged off to the house.

Frazer guessed that Winston was asking for Ella. And, remembering the veiled glance Corey and Ella had exchanged, Frazer was quite sure they had found some way to be alone together. With Winston already on the prod, Frazer decided to look for them. He wandered behind a

14

grove of trees and came around the far side of the barn. Moving toward the rear door, he turned the corner and stopped.

Ella and Corey were in an empty stall. They were locked in each other's arms. It was a long, passionate embrace. When at last Ella drew back she said to Corey: "Why didn't you kiss me inside?"

Corey smiled. It was a twisted, half-serious smile, diffident and uncaring. "I don't want an audience when I kiss you."

"Let's try another," Ella murmured.

Corey bent his head and claimed her lips again. When he'd had his fill of her he said: "Ella, I don't know when I'll ever get enough of you."

Ella's proud face seemed to shrivel. "Bill, why did I marry Van?"

"You know the answer better than I do."

"You don't even care," she accused.

"Sure I do." Corey's smile was constant. It seemed to be painted on his face. "Any time you tire of Winston I'll be around. You know where to find me."

Frazer hated the role of an eavesdropper so he retreated from the barn doorway. However, a chance glance toward the ranch house changed his mind again. Winston was tramping down the veranda steps. He swung around the side of the house, angling toward the rear yard.

Slipping quickly through the trees, Frazer gained the barn doorway again. He stepped inside.

"Better break it up," he said. "Winston's coming this way."

Ella pulled nervously away from Corey. With deft fingers she straightened her hair, smoothed out her dress.

"Thanks for the warning," she said to Frazer. "I'll go out the front way. You two duck out through the back."

"Hell, I'm not afraid of Winston," growled Corey.

15

"Please!" she said, coming close to Corey and gripping his arms. "Don't make it difficult for me. I'll find some way of seeing you."

Corey kissed her lightly. "If you don't, I will."

Ella turned and hurried along the length of the barn toward the half-open front door.

"Come on, Bill, the party's over," Frazer said, and led Corey out the rear door.

They circled through the brush that grew up close to the back wall of the barn, angling for Winston's corral beyond the bunkhouse. At that they were close enough to hear the brief exchange of conversation that ensued when Winston met Ella.

"Where were you?" Winston demanded.

"I wanted some air," she said.

"Where? In the barn?" There was a pause. When Ella didn't reply Winston went on doggedly. "I'll bet you were seeing Frazer again."

This time Ella's answer came back at Winston, swift and hard. "If you're so certain of that why did you ask me?"

"Keep away from him, Ella, or I'll kill him."

"That'll take a lot of doing."

If Winston replied to that taunt neither Frazer nor Corey heard it. They were moving farther away from the newlyweds all the time. When they emerged from the brush and struck along the pole corral, heading for the rope enclosure where they had left their saddlers, Winston and Ella were standing stiffly near the ranch-house veranda waving good-by to departing guests.

Frazer and Corey caught their mounts and climbed into their saddles. Squinting against the slanting rays of the hot afternoon sun blazing down out of a pale blue sky, Frazer said: "Going home, Bill?"

Corey grinned and shook his head. "No. I reckon I'll ride on into town and see what's doing."

Trotting beside his friend, Frazer made a caustic observation. "You're spending more time in Two Forks lately than on your ranch."

The blue in Corey's eyes turned to purple. "Hell, kid, you keeping tabs on me again?"

"Just hate to see your place go to pot."

"It's mine, Tom, so let me run it."

"That's just it. You don't run it."

Corey stopped his horse. He twisted in the saddle. His eyes flickered coldly at Frazer. Then he grinned. "Stop worrying." He jingled a few coins in his pocket. "A little poker never hurt anybody."

"It hasn't helped you any, Bill." Frazer hesitated before adding: "You still seeing Guy Thorpe?"

"Sure. What of it?"

"He's a hard case. Steer clear of him."

Corey's grin became labored. "Kid, I can take care of myself. Thorpe's all right. A little tough, maybe. That's all."

"What about the rustling?" Frazer queried.

"Hell, no one's ever caught him at it."

Frazer's control snapped. "Damn it, Bill, you're a fool. First Thorpe. Now Ella. They'll both bring you grief."

Corey's mouth hardened. "That's enough, kid. Let me pick my friends and run my life. So long."

Corey dug his spurs into the piebald gelding he was riding and sped off past the Circle W ranch house.

2   Harry Yorke, one of the Double-Y punchers, was waiting with Margo near the cottonwood grove when Frazer rode up. Yorke was a man in his middle thirties, mild-mannered and friendly. His unruly brown hair kept escaping from the loosely fitting sweatband of his sombrero. Yorke had the team of blacks hitched to the Double-Y buckboard and was mounted on his own saddle pony, waiting for orders.

"Tex and Hal go already?" Frazer asked.

"Yeah," said Yorke. "You need me for anything?"

"No. Better ride over to the River Bend line camp and keep an eye on that herd of prime Herefords. I'll send Tex over in the morning to give you a hand."

Yorke nodded, tipped his hat to Margo, and spurred away down the road. Frazer climbed down from his roan gelding. He led the horse to the tail gate of the wagon and looped the reins around it. Then he walked forward, heaved himself into the front seat, and freed the reins of the blacks from the whipstock. He turned to Margo sitting next to him and said, "Ready?"

She nodded. Frazer clucked to the team and they started off past the Circle W ranch house. Then Winston ran toward him. He waved his arm imperiously. "Hold it, Frazer."

The Double-Y ramrod pulled in the blacks. Winston

walked up to the buckboard. He gave Frazer a cheerless, unfriendly glance then spoke to Margo.

"Have you thought any more about my offer?"

"No, she hasn't, Winston," snapped Frazer.

Winston lifted his craggy head. His features squeezed into a red wedge of rage. "Do you own the Double-Y?" he demanded.

"No. But I run it."

Their eyes met, Winston's black as coal and with no light at all in them; Frazer's a frigid steel-blue, relentless and unfearing. Winston drew a heavy breath. He forced himself to look at Margo. "Does Frazer speak for you, Margo?"

The girl's lips pressed together. Her dislike for Winston was a live thing. She said shortly: "He does."

"I offered a fair price for the Double-Y," Winston persisted.

"Like hell you did," said Frazer.

Winston's heavy-set cheeks darkened but he ignored the ramrod. He kept hammering away at Margo. "You've still got a note at the bank."

"Ben Revere will give me a renewal on it if I need it," Margo said.

"Don't be too sure. Money's tight. What'll you do if Ben refuses to renew?" Winston's face was abruptly sly.

"We'll take care of that when the time comes."

Winston shrugged. "Suit yourself."

He retreated from the buckboard. Frazer watched his face for some sign of anger or disappointment. There was none. Winston had expected Margo's answer, then.

Oddly disturbed yet not knowing why, Frazer whipped the blacks into a fast run. The buckboard careened down the rutted road. Behind its rattling wheels rose a cloud of gray, finely powdered dust. Trees and brush sped by in a blur. Frazer and Margo were thrown from side to side and the vehicle rocked crazily in the ruts.

Then, after the blacks had taken the kinks out of their system and had slowed to a ground-eating trot, Margo swung toward Frazer. "What were you doing down at the barn?" she asked.

Frazer reddened in surprise. He hesitated, then said, "I was with Bill Corey."

"Ella was there too." Margo's tanned cheeks were pale now. "You can't leave her alone, can you?"

It was ironic, Frazer thought, how the people in Two Forks continued to link his name with Ella's. They all remembered that he and Ella had gone together for quite a while. No one suspected that Corey had long ago succeeded him in Ella's affections. Corey, careless as he was in many things, had been mighty secretive in his meetings with Ella. Of course he had been seen with Ella on occasion, but always these occurrences had the appearance of casual encounters.

"You got things all wrong," Frazer told Margo.

Margo looked fully at Frazer. She could knock a man down with her eyes or she could be all womanly and soft. Her eyes were not soft now; neither were they tender. "She's married now. I hoped you'd remember."

Frazer took her hand. "I'm not likely to forget."

Margo withdrew her hand. She trembled and looked off across the prairie. There was a fineness about her features that Frazer admired. During the past few months he had felt himself drawn to Margo. There was a strong pull to her personality. She was straightforward, never oblique. She had met her father's serious illness with fortitude. She had taken over the responsibility of the ranch and had tried to do a man's work in the saddle.

The hours they had spent out on the range together had brought a sense of warmth and completeness to

20

Frazer. Yet Margo had always maintained a certain reserve with him. He didn't at first know if it was because, technically, she was his boss. But lately it had occurred to him that Ella was the cause of it. Margo couldn't forget that he and Ella had once been very close.

He pulled the blacks to a halt.

"What are you stopping for?" Margo asked.

"It's time we got a few things straightened out between us," he murmured. "Like how I really feel about you and the Double-Y." He leaned toward her.

She pulled away. Her mouth was ridged with a strange tightness. "There's nothing to straighten out," she said.

"I'm afraid there is. When your father was taken ill two years ago I promised him I'd look after the ranch and you too. I reckon you'll agree that the ten months you spent in Frisco with him the Double-Y made money." Frazer's voice dropped and his features were sober and serious. "I don't reckon there's a thing I wouldn't do for you or the Double-Y."

Margo looked at him. He imagined a subtle softening of her eyes. Her presence beside him was a strong and compelling force. A wild impulse flashed through him. He wanted to take her in his arms.

"Why are you telling me all this?" she asked.

"Can't you guess?" he said. He made a half-turn toward her. Her nearness shook him up, leaving his nerves atingle.

For a moment Margo's composure broke. A ripple of emotion crossed her cheeks. Her eyes were abruptly caressing and intimate. The curve of her lips grew gentle and warm. Frazer put his arm around her. He tried to kiss her. But her lips avoided his and she pushed him roughly away.

"If you're trying to make love to me," she said bitterly, "this is neither the time nor the place for it." She slid to

21

the extreme end of the buckboard's seat. There was a taut breathlessness in her words. Her eyes, gray and narrow, were stricken and unrelenting.

Grimness touched Frazer's face. He pulled his arm back. The impact of her glance left him cold. He climbed down from the wagon. He went around to the tail gate and untied his roan. Then he vaulted into the saddle and rode up to Margo.

"Where are you going?" She was abruptly bewildered and frightened.

"To town," he said curtly. "You can take the buckboard back to the ranch."

"Corey again, I suppose," she said.

"No. Something else."

She waited for a fuller explanation. Frazer gave none. His face was hard set. He lifted his hat and rode away at a fast clip.

A few minutes before three o'clock he racked up his pony at the hitching rail in front of the Two Forks bank. Standing on the edge of the boardwalk to build a quirly, Frazer studied the town's main street. It was a wide thoroughfare, rutted by the steel tires of many wagons and pitted with numerous holes. A brisk wind out of the southwest agitated the loose gray soil on the road's surface and sent it whirling through space. Fine grains of sand pelted Frazer's face and whisked off the weathered frame walls of the ramshackle store buildings that lined both sides of the street.

Only a few people were abroad at this hour. The sun was hot. A purple haze shimmered above the ramparts of the Toulose Mountains off in the distance. The hostler at the livery barn halfway down the street sat in a rickety wooden chair tilted precariously on its rear legs, his back leaning against the wall.

Frazer jammed the cigarette in his mouth, lit it, and

drew a deep drag of smoke into his lungs. Four horses were tied to the hitching rail in front of the Maverick Saloon. A lonely nester wagon was drawn up close to the walk beside the Mercantile and a small stooped man was occupied with piling a sack of dried and tinned food in the wagon bed.

Frazer took another puff at his cigarette, held the smoke for a second or two, relishing its savor, before expelling it. Then he turned on his heel and walked into the bank.

It took him a moment to adjust his vision to the cool darkness of the room. There was no one at the single cashier's wicket. But the sound of his heels drumming on the floor pulled the bespectacled face of Jan Marvin, the cashier, into view.

"Ben in his office?" Frazer asked.

Marvin nodded. Then as Frazer moved past the wicket to a closed door marked private the cashier called: "Wait a minute. I'll see if he's free."

Frazer kept on. "Never mind," he said. "I'll see for myself."

Marvin came after him in a scuttling run. But Frazer beat him to the door. His hand turned the knob and he strode inside.

Ben Revere, a small, narrow-shouldered individual with pale cheeks and paler gray eyes, looked up from his desk in surprise at Frazer's unannounced entrance. He glared at Marvin and said: "I thought I told you that——"

"It's all right, Ben," Frazer interrupted. "Marvin's not to blame. I decided to walk in."

A red flush of anger stained Revere's thin, tight-skinned face. "Next time, see that you knock," he said coldly.

Frazer took a drag on his cigarette, blew the smoke

coolly across the desk toward Revere. The banker coughed as some of the smoke caught in his throat.

"I reckon any time I want to see you, Ben, I'll walk in," Frazer told him. Revere drew back in his chair. There was an unpleasant light in the ramrod's eyes he didn't like. Frazer said: "I came to see you about Margo's note."

An odd expression flickered in Revere's pale eyes. His answer was low and cautious. "What about it?"

"We're going to need more time."

Revere clasped his hands in front of him. He barely met Frazer's intent glance. "You can't have it."

Frazer's big blunt fingers crushed the cigarette in two. The burning tip scraped his palm. He cursed and dropped it to the floor. His heel ground it to shreds. "Why not?" he demanded harshly. "You agreed with Margo that if she needed more time you'd take care of her."

Revere looked nervous and apologetic. He unclasped his hands, began fumbling with the soiled white collar of his shirt. "Things have changed," he said lamely. "Money is tight."

"I've heard that before," snapped Frazer.

"What do you mean?"

Frazer ignored Revere's question. He said, "Now, let's have the real reason why you won't give Margo more time."

Dark lines of worry swam in the banker's eyes. He coughed nervously before venturing to speak. "I've told you. Money is tight. We have too many outstanding notes. The bank needs cash. It's been a hard year in the cattle business and——"

"All the more reason for you to stand behind the cowmen who are your livelihood," said Frazer relentlessly.

"Sorry, Frazer," said Revere. "The bank is holding everyone to the deadline of his note. If I make an exception with Margo——"

The rest was choked off as Frazer leaped around the desk and caught the banker's shirt front in one big fist. The force of his hold pulled the neckband of the shirt tightly around Revere's throat. The banker's eyes popped. Cold sweat oozed from his forehead. Frazer hauled him out of his chair.

"You still got Margo's note?" he asked.

Revere struggled ineffectually to get free. He flailed at Frazer with swinging arms. Frazer's grip tightened. He said savagely: "I want the truth, Revere, and I want it now. Did you sell Margo's note to Van Winston?"

Frazer had pulled the banker to a point within inches of his own face. Revere quailed at the cold fury he saw mirrored in Frazer's eyes. Weakly Revere nodded his head. Frazer pushed him backward. Revere toppled into his chair, carried it over backward, and crashed into the far wall of his office. He lay there, whimpering in terror, as Frazer towered over him.

"By God," Frazer said, "if you were any kind of a man I'd kill you." The ugly suspicion that had sprung into his mind after Winston had queried Margo about the Double-Y outfit was now an accomplished fact. Winston held the whip over Margo's head. Frazer went on: "Someday you're going to be run out of Two Forks on a rail. Why did you sell that note?"

Revere's face was twisted into a terrified grimace that filled Frazer with disgust. Revere babbled brokenly: "I—I told you. Things are tight. The—the bank over—over extended itself on loans. Winston offered me a good profit on the note. I—I just had to take it."

Frazer had enough. He couldn't trust himself any longer in the office with Revere. He hitched up his single gun belt and turned to the door. When he flung it open he

25

found Marvin, the cashier, standing on the far side. Marvin tried to back out of his path. Frazer hit him with his right shoulder, spun him against the side wall, and kept going to the street.

His rage remained with him during his brief walk down to the Maverick Saloon. Then near the hitch rack he paused to study the four ponies tied there. Three of the animals wore a Big T brand on their rumps. That meant Guy Thorpe, his foreman, Pole Richmond, and probably hard-case Ray Long were inside playing poker. The fourth horse carried a C-Minus brand—Bill Corey's iron.

Frazer's features immediately settled and his eyelids contracted. He wheeled across the walk, thrust his way past the bat-wing doors. Once inside the reek of stale whisky and sawdust smote his nostrils. He blinked in the gloom. A quick glance showed him that no one was at the bar except the bartender.

The four men whose horses he had identified were seated at a card table. Chips and money were piled in front of each player. There were two half-filled whisky bottles and several glasses on the table.

Frazer strode over to the players, somberly watching how the men paused to glance sharply at him over the rims of their cards. Pole Richmond's caustic, razor-edged voice broke the silence.

"Corey, here's your watchdog!"

Bill Corey, his back to the bat wings, swung half around. "Damn it, Tom," he said. "What are you doing in here?" His eyes were red-rimmed from drink. There was only a small stack of chips in front of him. He was in a black mood.

"You own the Maverick now, Bill?" Frazer asked idly.

But Frazer didn't look at Corey. His eyes rested on Pole Richmond, watching the Big T ramrod's cold, mirthless features. Richmond was two inches over six feet

26

and slender in the hips and shoulders. His face was gaunt and gray and unsmiling. There was a wiry, feline strength in his gangling frame. His hands were smooth and white like a gambler's. They hardly looked big enough to handle the two big .45 Colts that rode in hand-tooled leather holsters on each hip. Frazer knew better. Richmond was fast—devilishly fast with a gun. And he didn't require much provocation to use one.

A new voice—Guy Thorpe's this time—entered the conversation. "Maybe you'd like to sit in on the game."

Thorpe was a powerfully built man. His shoulders were solid and well-proportioned. His waist was lean and trim from long hours spent in the saddle. He had a long, hawk-nosed face and a mouth that was like a bar of gray steel against the brownish hue of his skin. Another two-gun man—a man who lived rashly, loved a fight, and played life's long gambles.

"You checking out?" Frazer asked him.

Thorpe, the dealer, flung two cards toward Corey at the latter's signal. Ray Long, a chunky, thick-lipped man with a pock-marked face and a narrow forehead to which black kinky hair clung in great tufts, bowed out. Pole Richmond took two cards. Then Thorpe doled out one card to himself. He picked up the five cards on the table, shuffled them briefly, fanned them out to look at them. Only then did he answer Frazer.

"Hell, no." He gestured to the pile of winnings in front of him.

"Then I won't buy in," Frazer told him.

Thorpe's irregular features took on weight. He shoved chips into the pot, then peered up at Frazer. "Maybe you're fussy about who you play poker with," he murmured.

A hard rancor spilled out of Frazer and touched the Big T cattleman. "Maybe I am."

27

The surfaces of Thorpe's gray-green eyes took on an unnatural sheen of light. Slowly he bunched his cards and laid them on the table top. He spread both hands out flat on the scarred wood. "I don't like your talk, Frazer," he said.

Hostility was a frigid wind blowing between these two men. The other players tensed. Richmond sucked in his lips. There was a ruddy shine to his cheeks.

Frazer never shifted his ground. His blue eyes were steady and unwavering as they met Thorpe's glance. When he spoke it was in a voice so soft and restrained that it held limitless menace. "I don't give a damn whether you like it or not!"

Richmond's cards dropped to the table. His hands moved back toward his guns. Thorpe's face turned darker and darker. The air in the room throbbed with thinly leashed violence. As Thorpe teetered on the edge of a break and Frazer coolly watched him, Corey suddenly banged his fist on the table.

"Lay off, Tom!" he growled. Then he looked at Thorpe. "And you—what are you so damned touchy about?"

"Shut up, Corey," said Thorpe. "Maybe your friend wants to make something out of this." Thorpe's narrow-lidded stare switched to the redheaded Double-Y ramrod.

The reckless mood clung to Frazer. He stood with his hands at his sides. His indolence in front of the three Big T riders was a measure of his contempt for them. Yet none of them were fools enough to think Frazer was not ready to swing into action. They knew how dangerous he could be. He had hell in his neck and hell in the one holster he wore on his right hip.

"Long as you're dealing," Frazer said, "I'll let you call this play."

Worry glinted briefly in Bill Corey's eyes. "Cut it out,

Tom," he said. His voice was thick from the liquor he had consumed. He dug his fingers into the meager stack of chips before him and pushed four of them out to the middle of the table. "Let's play poker," he said, and added to Thorpe, who had opened the pot, "I'm raising you."

Thorpe sat taut and still in his chair for several long seconds. Then he picked up his cards again and looked at Pole Richmond. Richmond grinned carelessly, thumbed some chips toward the pot, and said, "Twenty dollars better."

Thorpe added some chips to the pile in the center. "I'll see you, Pole."

It was up to Corey now. Anger and indecision ridged his cheeks. He had been holding three aces but hadn't bettered his hand on the draw. Frazer saw his hand linger over the two remaining chips in front of him. Then with a curse he flung his hand into the discard.

Richmond and Thorpe exchanged grins. The Big T ramrod turned up three kings. Thorpe, however, had come up with a jack full. He reached for the chips in the center of the table.

"Your luck hasn't changed, Bill," Frazer observed. "How long have you been losing like this?"

Corey's bitterness tugged at his lip corners. "It's my money," he said.

"Sure it is," Frazer agreed, "but I hate to see you throwing it away."

He wheeled away from the table and walked over to the bar to order a drink. The bartender poured a whisky for him. He picked up the glass, drank half of it, and waited for the liquid to set up its accustomed warm glow in his belly.

Corey had changed in the last few months, grown more morose. His gay moods were rare these days. He drank

29

more and gambled more. The fact that he seldom won at poker made Frazer wonder how long it would be before his friend was flat broke. Lingering by the bar, he watched Corey finally win a pot on his own deal. The deck then passed to Pole Richmond.

The ramrod shuffled the cards expertly, doled them out. Thorpe opened and everybody played along. On the draw Thorpe took two cards, Ray Long one, and Corey one. Frazer stode idly across the room as Richmond threw two cards into the discard, set his hand down, and quickly dealt himself two others. His fingers were deft and fast. Perhaps it was the angle at which the ceiling lamp above the table cast light upon Richmond. Or perhaps Richmond's fingers fumbled just slightly in the deal. In any event, Frazer saw him deal the second card off the bottom of the deck.

He lunged toward Richmond. "Hold it!" he ordered.

Thorpe threw down his hand and glared. "Stay out of this, Frazer!"

Frazer ignored him. His eyes were on Richmond. "You always deal off the bottom of the deck?"

"Frazer, that's a damned lie!" Richmond roared. He dropped the deck on the table. Hot blood pumped into his head.

Frazer hit Corey with his next words. "Bill, you poor fool. Where are your eyes?"

Richmond and Thorpe went for their Colts simultaneously. Fast as they were, Frazer was even faster. With a lightning motion he flung his whisky, glass and all, full at Thorpe's face. Thorpe's fingers were closing around his gun butt when the burning liquor splashed into his eyes. The empty glass cascaded off his cheek and struck the table. Thorpe yelled in pain. He pawed at his eyes.

Frazer had already turned away from him. He leaped at Richmond. A short right to the point of Richmond's jaw spun the Big T man off balance. He pitched against an empty table in back of him, struck it with the lower part of his back, and carried it down to the floor with him. He lost his right-hand Colt, groped frantically for the weapon in his other holster. And into the din of the falling table rose Thorpe's screaming voice.

"Gun him down, Ray!"

3   Ray Long never did get a chance to go into action. Corey, red-eyed and slow-witted from all the drinking he had done, nevertheless rallied his senses sufficiently to slam Long's Colt out of his hand just as he was lining the sights on Frazer's back.

"Keep out of this, Ray!" Corey warned. His own gun nestled snugly in his palm now. He retreated from the table. "That goes for you, too, Guy. Stay away from your hog-leg!"

Tears of pain streaming from his reddened eyes, Thorpe fixed his savage attention on Corey. "I hope you know what you're doing."

"I know this," snapped Corey. "If there's going to be a fight it'll be a fair one—even up with no back shooting!"

Frazer was only dimly aware of the action going on behind him. The heat of his fierce temper had taken complete hold of him. He had pulled all the stops. Rage was in him. It needed release.

He saw Richmond's left hand dig for the holster on his left hip. One rapid lunge carried him over to the ramrod. His boot toe caught Richmond's wrist as the latter flicked the weapon out of leather. The gun went skidding across the floor. Then Richmond's groping hand trapped Frazer's ankle. A savage pull hauled Frazer off his feet. He fell in a heap. Richmond scrambled on top of him. A wild, sledging blow nailed the side of Frazer's head. Then the Big T foreman's thumb jammed into Frazer's left eye. Hot pain seared Frazer's eyeball. He struck Richmond's hand away. He chopped a blow to Richmond's cheek. He wrenched his body to one side, spilling Richmond to the floor.

They rolled along the rough boards, punching and jabbing at each other. Their labored breathing and the sodden thump of fists finding a mark on flesh and bone were the only sounds in the saloon.

Frazer suddenly found himself on top of Richmond. He pummeled him with both hands, swinging in measured fashion for Richmond's face. Once his knuckled fist connected with the Big T foreman's nose. He felt the cartilage flatten beneath his knotted fingers. Blood squirted over his knuckles. Richmond gasped in pain. He drove his knee into the pit of Frazer's stomach.

The breath rushed out of Frazer. Again Richmond's pointed knee slammed into his belly. Frazer was propelled backward. His heavy shoulders struck the legs of the table at which Richmond and his friends had been playing poker. The table keeled over on its side. Chips, glasses, cards, and the two liquor bottles skidded to the floor and shattered. Whisky ran a brown trail along the scuffed puncheons.

Somewhere behind him Frazar heard Corey yell. "Stand back, Guy. Give them room!"

Then Richmond was rising and leaping at him. Frazer, still suffering from those two thrusts of Richmond's knees, retreated in an attempt to recapture his wind. His foot slipped in the spilled whisky. He struggled to keep his balance, arms flailing. With his guard down he was a fair target for a whistling right-hand uppercut. The shock of the punch traveled from his jaw, up along the nerves of his face to the top of his skull. It numbed him. A reddish haze gyrated before his eyes. He went down, rolled over on his back. Immediately he felt a sharp sliver of broken glass slice through his shirt.

Thinking only of this new pain, he was hardly ready for the Big T ramrod's next move. Richmond followed him quickly. He jumped toward Frazer, plainly intent on tromping him. Frazier writhed away. But one heavy boot caught him high on the chest. Agony cut a hard track across his nerves. It was like a grinding weight, beating all through his tissues with a slow and calculated torture.

Richmond's cruel features burned with an ugly frenzy. He sensed that victory was in his grasp. Hate was a corroding flux in his mind. It drove him at Frazer again.

Frazer recognized his danger. The muscles of his jaw hardened against the pain that still beat in pulsating waves through his chest. He caught the leg of a chair in one hand. Flat on his back, he brought his arm forward and hurled the chair in Richmond's path.

The chair hit Richmond directly below the knees. He tried to halt his forward lunge. He could not. The chair bounced off his legs. Richmond pitched forward on his face.

It was just the respite Frazer needed. He climbed to his feet. His long red hair hung down across his eyes. The raw, warm taste of blood was in his mouth. Every breath he sucked into his lungs brought fresh pain. He saw that Richmond was rising. He saw that Richmond was still full of fight. And at this moment, as had happened on other occasions, Frazer's savage, indomitable will took hold.

Born and bred in a hard land where a man's power to resist often meant the difference between life and death, he had no illusions about Richmond's intentions. The Big T foreman meant to kill him. This land and the men in it were nurtured in brutality, drilled in the vicious art of destruction. If you didn't fight back, you were doomed.

Hurt though he was, Frazer met Richmond's next rush with a counterattack that surprised the Big T ramrod. Frazer took a hard punch to the temple, blocked another lead on his forearm. Then he struck back with two sharp lefts to Richmond's face. The second hit Richmond's already bleeding nose, spreading a claret streak all over Richmond's mouth and chin.

Richmond stopped, covered up momentarily. Frazer led with a short, flicking left to the head. Richmond swung a right that missed. Then Frazer slipped inside, countering with a left to the nose again. He drove two more lefts to the stomach, then a pile-driving right to the jaw. He pushed Richmond back, hit him once more with his right. Richmond went back on his heels. He hit the floor amid the litter of broken glasses and the shattered whisky bottle.

"Get in there and fight, Pole!" Thorpe raged.

Richmond's features were a livid mask of blood. One eye was puffed. He was breathing heavily through his mouth. Frazer waited for him to get up. He, too, was breathing hard. But his strength had come back and the fever of fighting once more was boiling inside him.

"Got enough, Pole?" he asked when Richmond didn't immediately rise.

"Not yet," Richmond rasped, and lunged up from the floor.

Lamplight flickered dully on the jagged surface of the broken whisky bottle he now held in his right hand. His fingers were curled around the neck. The lower half of the bottle terminated in a series of uneven razor-edged points. It was a wicked weapon. It was more deadly than a knife. It could tear a man's insides out.

Corey's voice roared a warning: "Richmond, put that bottle down or I'll drill you!"

But there was no time for a shot even if Corey had

35

wanted to fire. Richmond flung himself at Frazer. The shattered bottle cut a whistling arc through the air as it drove at Frazer's vitals. Frazer ducked under Richmond's sweeping arm. One of the jagged tines of gláss raked the top of Frazer's shoulder, ripping his shirt and planing a shallow gash in the flesh.

Then Frazer came in close to Richmond. His left hand caught Richmond's right wrist. He flung his right arm around Richmond's waist. He got a solid purchase in the ramrod's belt. With a tremendous heave he lifted Richmond off his feet, swayed in a half circle. Then he hurled Richmond against the bar.

It was an amazing feat of strength. Richmond struck the edge of the bar with a jolt that knocked down a row of glasses and threatened to uproot the bar from the floor. The jagged whisky bottle flew from Richmond's hand. As he hung there, half-bent across the bar, Frazer moved in for the finish. A solid left to the heart pulled Richmond's guard down. Then a pulverizing right slammed to the point of his jaw. His eyes glazed over and he slowly slid to the floor, one arm dangling loosely over the stained brass footrail.

Frazer let his arms fall wearily to his sides. Now that the fight was over, all the pleasure that action always gave him washed out of him. He looked down at Richmond's battered, bloody features and experienced an odd sensation of distaste. He turned away from the bar. He saw Corey still holding Thorpe and Long at bay.

"Thanks for the hand, Bill," he murmured. He picked up his hat which had fallen to the floor, clamped it on his head.

"You damn fool," growled Corey, "you almost bought yourself a shot in the back."

Frazer glanced at Thorpe and Long. Their antagonism was a muddy, virulent stain in their eyes. Thorpe's brows

36

were drawn together. The thick vein in his neck stood out like a steel cable. The light in his eyes was yellow and strange.

"Get out!" he ordered in a voice that was almost unrecognizable because of the passion that throbbed in it.

Frazer wiped the palms of his hands on his pants. "When I'm damned good and ready," he replied. Then he turned to Corey. "Maybe you've had enough poker for a spell."

Corey's face turned sullen. His eyes shuttled to Thorpe, then back to Frazer. "Skip the sermon, kid."

Frazer said quietly, "That the way you want it, Bill?"

"Yeah."

Thorpe cut in again. He was bent a little at the shoulders. There was venom in his eyes and venom in his talk. "Frazer, don't ever get in my way again."

Frazer's blue eyes flashed. "How about now, Thorpe?"

"I'll pick my time," Thorpe said. "One thing is sure. You'll pay for this. And if I ever see you on Big T range consider yourself fair game for my gun."

"What's the matter? Are you afraid I might see some strange cattle eating Big T grass?"

Thorpe's lips twitched in rage. "Just what do you mean by that?"

"I reckon you can guess," said Frazer bluntly.

"That's the same as calling me a rustler," Thorpe growled. He was burning up. His hatred for Frazer at this moment formed into something ugly and devastating. "No man can put a rustler tag on me without answering for it."

Thorpe's hand slowly dropped to his holstered Colt. The bitter wine of killing fermented in his brain. His glance was like a white-hot brand searing Frazer. But the redhead stood immobile. He returned Thorpe's gaze with an unwinking steadiness that was disconcerting. Frazer's

37

whole life had been built on one premise: No surrender and no compromise. This stern creed of his showed now in every inch of him.

"I'm here to answer right now, Guy," he murmured gently. "Make your play or shut up."

The challenge was like a slap in the face. A more headstrong, unthinking man than Thorpe might have been goaded into action. But Thorpe only shook his head fiercely like a bulldog worrying a bone. His features changed from white to red to purple. Ray Long watched him, ready to go for his gun and join Thorpe if the latter elected to draw.

"Not now," Thorpe finally said. The words were so thick they almost bogged down in his throat. "Your number's coming up soon. Just remember that."

"In other words, watch my back," said Frazer with icy scorn. "Good enough." He paused briefly, then added, "This is for you. Someday I figure on finding out how you make your money. If it's the way I think, Two Forks won't be big enough to hold the both of us."

He strode to the saloon door. There he turned, looked over at Corey, and said, "See you soon, Bill." Then he shouldered through the bat wings and vanished into the late-afternoon sunlight.

After he had gone Thorpe swung his heavy, ponderous body around to face Bill Corey. "Corey," he said savagely, biting off each word as if it left an acid taste in his mouth, "the next time you interfere in my business I'll kill you."

Corey was cold sober now. His eyes were still red-veined from the liquor he had drunk. But he was thinking clearly and he was fully braced for trouble. "You were fixing to plug Tom in the back," he said.

Thorpe's answer was quick and curt. "He asked for it."

"That so?" The red in Corey's eyes deepened. He met

Thorpe's words head on. "Well, get this. I take your dirty money and I ride with your bunch but I've told you before to keep hands off Tom. He's my friend."

"Hell of a friend you are."

"That's my affair."

Thorpe switched his attention to Pole Richmond, who groaned and began to move. Then he jerked his head at Long. "Get a pail of water out in back and throw it on Pole. We've got to be riding soon."

Long threw a significant look at Corey. "You're all right?" he asked Thorpe.

The Big T owner laughed harshly. "Hell, yes."

Long walked to the rear door of the saloon and went out. Thorpe, now oddly mollified, said to Corey: "I wonder how Frazer would like it if he knew you helped steal that last bunch of Margo Nash's cattle?"

"Are you expecting to tell him?" Corey's question was weighted and dangerous.

"He'll figure it out someday," Thorpe replied.

"When he does, your number will be up, Guy. If Tom figures that far he'll know who I'm riding for. You'll be top man on his list. That won't be good for you."

Thorpe sneered. All his confidence, all his arrogance had returned. "I'm not worried. I'll get him first. Fact is, he's on his way out now."

Corey's jaw hardened. He moved a stride nearer to Thorpe. "What I said still goes, Guy. Keep your hands off Tom. If anything happens to him I'm coming after you."

A wave of dark blood rolled up in Thorpe's fleshy cheeks. "Don't try to threaten me," he warned. "You spoke about taking my dirty money. Sure it's dirty. But I notice you're hungry for it. You're nothing but a two-timing two-bit cowman. Not a rider in the Big T crew has any use for you. Most of them are outlaws. But not one of them is cutting his best friend's throat behind his back like you are. Think that over. And remember, if a man gets in my way he goes—with a bullet or with anything that happens to be handy. That holds for Tom Frazer."

Thorpe turned insolently away from Corey then, and watched the back door swing open to admit Ray Long with a pail of water.

4   After Margo Nash and Tom Frazer left the Circle W ranch, taking the Double-Y crew with them, the wedding celebration broke up rapidly. Ben Revere, the banker, got his buggy, stopped by to wish Ella and her new husband good luck, and rode off in the direction of town. Others followed in swift succession as if, now that the ice had been broken, they could not go quickly enough.

Ella and Van Winston stood side by side at the foot of the veranda bidding their guests good-by. Buckboards and buggies rolled by in brief whorls of dust. There were perfunctory waves of the hand, awkward utterances of thanks. Some few riders on horseback did not even bother with those formalities.

As the guests went and the crowd in the front yard dwindled, Ella's spirits sank. For a time the excitement of the wedding had buoyed her up. She had been the center of attraction, the cynosure of secretly admiring eyes. But now everyone was going. In just a little while she would be left alone with Van Winston. The thought was frightening. She felt a quiver run along her flesh. She knew with a dismal and unutterable feeling that this day was one she would regret for the rest of her life.

One of the hill ranchers drove past in a buckboard. The man's prim wife sat beside him. The woman waved to Ella. There was no word, not even a smile of warmth. And Ella realized, for the first time, how much alone she would be at the Circle W. She had no particular friends in Two Forks. And she saw with total clarity that Winston was likewise friendless.

The ranchwoman's eyes lingered on Ella's face for just a brief instant. But it was time enough for Ella to detect a note of pity in the frank glance. Suddenly Ella realized that they knew—all these women and perhaps their men too—that her marriage was a sham and a farce. They understood it was not a union compounded of love and affection. For Ella it was a marriage of convenience—an escape from poverty, a desperate groping for security. For Winston it was a marriage of convenience, too, but on a different level, a level that had its roots in physical appetite and the overbearing pride of possession.

Winston's gruff voice broke into Ella's reverie. "What are you so glum about?" he queried.

She looked up at him and away. "They're all going," she said.

"That's good," Winston grunted. "Their bellies are full at my expense. Let them go home where they belong."

Ella swung half-around. She spoke coldly. "So you begrudge them a wedding meal."

He slipped his arm around Ella's waist. She tried to draw away. But the last of the ranch buckboards was rattling by so she smiled at the departing guests and suffered Winston's arm to remain where it was.

When the wagon had passed down the road and the last of the horsemen had gone off Winston pulled her closer. "What's eating you? You've got what you wanted."

"Have I?" she asked quickly, then stopped as his eyes bored into her like a deep drill.

"Frazer again," he snapped. His mouth was a rigid

42

gray streak, the broad lips firmly anchored together. They parted slightly to permit his next words to slip past. "Better forget him. You're married to me now."

Once again Ella experienced a shock of surprise that Winston linked her only with Tom Frazer. No one seemed to suspect her relationship with Bill Corey. Perhaps it was because most of her earlier meetings with Corey had been carried out in a clandestine fashion during the period Frazer was courting her. Though she had been seen from time to time afterward with Corey they had gone on meeting secretly and at night.

"Tom doesn't mean anything to me now," she told Winston.

"That's good," Winston said. He turned her around so that she faced the house. "Let's go inside."

She held back, feeling her heart beat like a trip hammer inside her breast. A wave of helplessness and fright swept her. She dreaded the hours that lay ahead of her.

When she had at first accepted Winston's offer of marriage she had felt no qualms about her action. She had had enough of the humiliation of proverty and miserable living. There hadn't ever been much happiness or light in her life. She could remember going from one dirt farm to another. She remembered how her mother had worked her way to the grave and how her father had drunk up the little money he earned from grubbing in the earth. There had been days on end of wondering where her next meal was coming from. She'd had enough of that. Anything was better—even marriage to a man she secretly detested.

That was what she had thought. But now that it was done—now that there was no going back, she was no longer sure. The pressure of Winston's hand on her elbow, the hungry insistence that flamed in his heavy-lidded eyes warned her what to expect.

"Don't tell me you're bashful," Winston chided. His words mocked her. "Or should I tell you how much I love you?" His taunting smile raked up her feelings, bringing anger.

"Don't bother," Ella told him curtly as she allowed herself to be pushed toward the veranda steps. At the top of the steps she added: "It wouldn't mean anything to either of us."

Winston led her to the front door. He grasped the knob, pulled the door toward him. When she moved in front of him to pass into the now empty living room he said: "That's right. It was a business deal. You wanted my money and the prestige that goes with the Circle W. I wanted you and all that goes with a pretty woman."

She halted beside the wide leather couch. Her right hand clenched as she whirled around. "Let's not talk about it."

A nasty, indefinable sound issued from Winston's throat. "What shall we talk about? Tom Frazer?"

Ella looked closely at Winston. She noted his crass, heavy features, the small dark eyes that were never pleasant, and decided she did not like what she saw. There was something coarse and secretly evil about this man. She wondered that she had never noticed it before.

"Not unless you do," she retorted.

"Maybe you find him more interesting."

"You're the one that's saying it," Ella snapped, thinking not of Frazer but of Corey with a deep pain that seared her like a live flame.

"And I'll say something else"—Winston's arm went possessively around Ella—"you've played the field and you've kissed your share of men. But from now on it's me you'll be kissing."

His head lowered. He found her lips. They were cool and unresponsive. For answer he held her more tightly,

44

having his way with her mouth and taking his own deliberate time. He felt her arms bunch against him and she
shoved him away.

There was a shocked, half-frightened look in her face,
and anger whipped tongues of flame all over her body.

"What's the matter?" he asked. "Don't you like it?"

Ella backed away from him. Winston followed, grinning like a huge cat. She stopped when she felt a table at
her back. A cold, inpalpable dread gripped her. He was
watching her like a hawk, enjoying every moment of this
scene. He was like a hunter stalking prey. An aching anxiety swelled in Ella's throat.

Winston reached for her again. Even the touch of his
hand upon her arm filled her with revulsion. His palm
was damp and clammy. There was an oily shine of sweat
on his cheeks. He was breathing hard. He was smiling.
But it was a smile without humor. A smile that had her
own destruction in it.

When she didn't answer her said, "Might as well start
getting used to me. I'm going to want a lot of attention."

She was afraid to give him her lips again and equally
afraid not to. Her heart was like a stone. He claimed her
again. And his mouth was like the rest of him, arrogant
and demanding and drawing the life out of her.

The slamming of the door behind them put an end to
the embrace. Winston turned, dropping his arms. Ella
sagged against the table. She put her hands to her throbbing temples and saw Jess Engel, the Circle W foreman
standing at the edge of the veranda.

"Get out, Jess," Winston ordered. "Can't you see I'm
busy acting like a husband?"

Engel tried on a grin. It didn't fit. He was a dour-faced,
swarthy-skinned individual. Tall, loose-limbed, and lean-
hipped, he had the typical build of a cowpuncher. He always wore a gray shirt and yellow neckerchief. There was

little sentiment in him, and he treated the Circle W crew harshly and unfeelingly. Only to Winston did he show a sullen, grudging respect mixed with a vague kind of fear.

"We're due to ride out to meet——" he began.

"I know," Winston cut in swiftly. "Clear out. I'll be with you in a little while." He slanted a mocking glance at Ella.

Engel's eyes traveled briefly up and down Ella's shapely figure, then turned away. It was a completely dispassionate survey. He said finally: "I'll wait for you at the corral," and walked away.

When he had gone Winston turned back to Ella. If he noticed how white and still she was, he did not show it by any break in his expression. He said abruptly: "Now we can get back to our personal business."

Ella drew away from him. Her lips writhed as she said: "Not now, Van." Desperation squirmed in her voice. "I really should help Mrs. Loring clean up the things from the table outside."

It was a way out—an avenue of escape. But Winston had other ideas. "She gets paid for doing that."

Ella put her hands out. She flattened them against Winston's chest. "It's too much for Mrs. Loring to handle all by herself," she said. Her voice was almost a sob.

"Damn Mrs. Loring!" Winston growled. "Think of your obligations to me. If it hadn't been for me your old man would have lost his two-bit farm. As I remember, I paid all his debts before he was killed in that landslide on the Dunbar road."

Ella met his anger with equal force. Anything, she thought, just so she blunted the edge of his crude wants. "You hounded Dad enough—and all because he had the gumption to farm ground you've always claimed but don't really own."

"This is cow country. It's time you realized that. Nesters have no place here. As for the land, I don't have to own it. I take what I need for my cows."

The clatter of horses galloping across the yard clawed at Winston's attention. He glanced at an ancient wall clock near the rough-hewn fireplace, then turned and went out the door, not looking at her. Once outside, he hurried to the corral.

Engel jumped down from the top bar of the corral as Winston approached. The ramrod slid into the saddle of a rangy piebald. Len Sterling, another puncher similar in build to Engel but more gaunt of face, was already mounted. He bent forward to free the reins of a roan gelding from the corral bar and flip them to Winston.

Winston swung up into the saddle. He waited for Sterling and Engel to range beside him, then led the way out of the ranch yard. They followed the wagon road for a half mile. Reaching a point where a hard-packed dirt trail wandered off to the right at a sharp tangent, Winston left the road.

The trail took them immediately into higher country. For the first mile or two they traversed a series of terraced meadows covered with a strong growth of grama grass. Here they flushed several bands of Circle W cows. Gradually stunted clumps of brush began to appear, then a few trees. Afterward the trees thickened and the way wound through a deep avenue in the pines.

Winston remained in front. He had nothing to say to Engel and Sterling. And neither of the two punchers felt impelled to attempt conversation.

Emerging from the pines, Winston entered upon a wide, flat plateau. Here Engel and Sterling drew abreast of him. The sun, losing some of its intense heat, slowly drifted downward in the western sky. A film of dust coated all the bushes. The only sound was the jingle of bit chains, the scuff of a horse's shoe on flinty rock, and the squeak of saddle leather as one of the riders changed position.

The mesa came to an end, narrowing and dropping into a funnel-like canyon that sliced through a high rock battlement. Once out of the defile they hit rolling country again, and Winston gave the spurs to his horse, whipping away at a fast clip.

They traversed a dry arroyo, skirted a boulder field that seemed out of place in this land of grass and wooded hills. Another swift mile brought them within sight of a pine-clad ridge.

The trail climbed the slope in a straight line. Winston hit the grade without any slackening of pace. Near the top of the knoll he curveted his mount sharply to the right and plunged headlong into the brush. A low branch slapped at his hat. He ducked and kept on. The horse fought his way through the tangle, making a great racket of it. Behind him Engel cursed as the branch that swiped at Winston's sombrero caught the foreman full in the face and nearly unseated him.

Abruptly the trees gave way, and Winston rode into a shadowy park. The ground was carpeted with pine needles and dried cones. A few deadfalls littered the area along with an occasional weather-rotted stump covered with moss and lichens.

Winston halted. He flung an impatient glance around the clearing. "They're late again," he said.

Engel hooked a chaps-clad leg over his saddle horn. "Porbably got delayed in town," he ventured.

The Circle W owner climbed down from the saddle. Once more he looked all around the clearing. He strode up to one of the dead-falls. He prodded it with his boot toe, watching patches of bark peel off the trunk. Then he came back to his horse and loosened the saddle girth.

Engel remained indolent and completely at ease. He

fashioned a quirly with a deftness born of much practice. He thrust the cylindrical tube of tobacco in his mouth, lit the end, and took a deep drag on it.

Fifteen minutes went by. Winston's impatience grew. He finally tightened the cinch again and climbed back into the saddle. "By God, if they're not here soon——"

He broke off as the sound of riders crashing through trees reached him in the dead silence of the pine park. Facing around to the east, he waited with set, truculent cheeks until three horsemen pushed into view. At the head of the group was Guy Thorpe. Behind him rode Ray Long. In the rear was the tall, battered shape of Pole Richmond.

Winston pinned his outraged glance on Thorpe. "Where the hell were you? We've been here close to thirty minutes."

"Got delayed in town," Thorpe replied.

"You spend too damn much time in Two Forks," Winston told him.

Thorpe's eyes lit up. His mouth pinched inward at the corners. "Since when are you regulating my hours?"

Winston's thick brows gathered in a dark frown. "There's work to be done."

"More dirty work?"

"Yeah. But there's money in it."

Thorpe grimaced angrily. "Sure, but you keep your nose clean."

"Got any complaints?" Winston demanded. His broad shoulders stirred under the tight span of his shirt. Dark eyes that were harsh and unsparing skewered the other man. Thorpe let a shrug be his reply. Winston's attention slid away from the Big T owner, lingered briefly on Ray Long, and ultimately came to rest on Richmond. "What happened to friend Richmond? Looks as if he got in the way of a cattle stampede."

49

Thorpe turned to the lanky Big T ramrod. One side of Richmond's face was swollen. His left eye was nearly closed and the lid had turned purple. Dried blood caked his nostrils. His upper lip was split. Morose and solemn and nursing a resentment that would gradually turn into almost diabolical hatred, Richmond remained silent.

"Tom Frazer horned into a poker game me and the boys were having," Thorpe finally explained. "There was trouble."

"I can see that." Winston laughed. His long upper lip curled in disdain. "No need to guess who came out at the short end." Richmond lifted his head, glared at the Circle W boss, but said nothing. "What were you and Long doing?"

"Corey was there too," said Thorpe. "He tossed in on Frazer's side." Quickly he gave an account of the saloon fight.

Again Winston laughed. "Richmond can't forget he was once a tinhorn. Serves him right." The Circle W owner had a sudden thought. "Sounds like Corey is getting out of hand. Maybe it's time to ditch him."

"He's still got his uses," Thorpe insisted.

"I don't like it. He and Frazer are too thick."

"Corey still needs money. And there's more of it in night-hawking other gents' cows than doing chores on his own place."

"And Frazer?" Winston's question held an insidious note.

For the first time Pole Richmond spoke. "Leave him to me."

"That sounds funny as hell coming from you."

"He's my meat, I tell you," Richmond said doggedly. His mouth was a thin gash against his bruised, malevolent face.

Thorpe cuffed his hat back on his head. "All right,

50

Van. What's your ticket? Another raid on the Double-Y?"

"Yeah," said Winston. "I want you to hit Margo's River Bend line camp. She's got some prime Herefords up that way. Get them."

"All right." Thorpe lifted his reins. "Guess we'll drift."

Winston held up his hand. "One more thing." A faint, hard amusement flickered in his dark eyes. "Starting with this raid I'll cut in on your take at the other end."

"You will like hell!" snapped Thorpe. He dropped the reins.

Jess Engel immediately let his reins slide along the mane of his horse. His hand fell to his thigh and stayed there, the fingers spread out and nervously tense.

"You've got objections?" asked Winston, his words oddly mild.

"You're damned right I have," Thorpe came back. He was leaning forward, his face very intense. "You said you were only interested in grass and water. The cattle are mine. That's been our deal all along."

Grimness touched Winston's features with iron. "Well, I'm changing the deal. From now on I cut in."

"You'll cut into a piece of hell," Thorpe told him. His voice was steady, but furious emotion lay behind it.

For the space of a few seconds no one moved. Richmond's horse snorted. There was a creak of saddle leather as Sterling straightened. Tides of warning plucked at the jangled nerves of all these men. Bleak lines bracketed Thorpe's lips. His body knotted up over the mane of his horse and red flecks of rage burst like rockets in his eyes.

"Did you ever figure," he went on with a stark and menacing compulsion, "that I've got enough men riding for the Big T to wipe out your ranch if I felt like it?"

Winston's teeth showed in a soundless snarl. The killing urge was in him. It was in all of them. A wrong word, a sudden movement would touch off an explosion. There

51

wasn't much loyalty or trust among their kind. Their relation was built on greed and crooked profit. It was an unholy alliance that would endure only as long as they proved useful to each other.

"Don't ever try it," said Winston.

Thorpe's hand was an inch nearer his holstered gun. Rashness prodded him like a knife pricking his flesh. "I could kill you now."

Winston regarded him with cool contempt. "The odds are even. Three to three. But I wonder if Richmond is at his best right now. While you're plugging me, what do you figure Engel and Sterling would be doing?" Winston paused an instant, and his expression grew sardonic. "Besides, the day I die you'll be finished in Two Forks."

"You scare me," Thorpe told him with a brittle laugh.

"It's something to think about," Winston said. "Revere at the bank is holding some papers of mine in his private safe. He's got instructions to open them up when I die. Among those papers are a few items about you, Guy." The Circle W rancher's mouth thinned out and a wicked grin tugged at his upper lip. "Sheriff Landon might be interested to know you're wanted for two killings up in Idaho."

Thorpe's cheeks whitened. A string of savage curses poured from him. "You're lying, Winston." His talk was all bluster. There was no conviction in the words.

Winston didn't even bother to answer him. He reverted to his original demand. "You take orders from me, Thorpe. And you run your Big T outfit just as long as I feel like letting you run it. Remember that. As I said, I cut in on all future deals you make on stolen beef. And that means the profits from those Double-Y cows you'll be going after tonight."

Richmond's dull, lethal glance went from Winston to Thorpe. The Big T owner was all hunched up with rage.

It twisted his craggy face into a gray, wrinkled mask. He couldn't talk, he was so mad. Finally he jerked his horse around, nodded curtly to Richmond and Long, and spurred toward the trees.

5   Tom Frazer rode out of Two Forks as if a high wind had taken hold of him and was shoving him along. The tumult of feelings that whirled inside him was a nagging pressure that could only be relieved by some additional outburst of energy.

He kept his horse at a full gallop for two miles before an element of calmness came to him. Then he pulled the speeding pony down to a trot. By that time he had already swung off the main road at a sharp angle and was following a side trail that would eventually bisect the road to the county seat at Dunbar.

He started to turn back, then changed his mind, deciding that he would stop off at Sam Bassett's outfit to ask Bassett if he'd been bothered by rustlers lately. He hadn't had the opportunity to broach the subject to Bassett during the brief wedding celebration at the Circle W.

Now as he jogged along the lifting trail past dusty green clumps of thorny brush he considered, as he had considered many times in recent weeks, his relationship with Bill Corey. There had been a time when they had been inseparable, riding the hills together, going on antelope hunts in the Indian Head Mountains, helling around in the saloons of Two Forks.

That had all changed several months ago. There were two reasons for the change. Both reasons were a source of

54

unhappiness and concern to Frazer. The first and foremost was Ella Land. He and Ella and Bill Corey had had lots of fun together at dances and ranch barbecues. But always it had been Frazer whom Ella had favored. Gradually Corey had stepped out of the picture, leaving a clear field to Frazer. At least, that's what Frazer and everyone else on the range had thought until the afternoon Frazer found Ella and Corey together at the abandoned Loon Peak line camp in a thick stand of pines bordering the Double-Y outfit and Corey's own two-bit spread.

In the short interval before breaking in on them Frazer had overheard enough of their talk to know that they had been meeting secretly for a number of weeks. And the way Ella had clung to Corey in a hot, passionate embrace told him where her feelings really lay.

The trail Frazer followed lifted over a ridge, dropped down a wooded slope already traced with the lengthening shadows of late afternoon. He recalled, as if it were only yesterday, the way rage had driven him that day. He had gone completely wild, lunging at Corey with both arms swinging. He had wanted to batter Corey to a pulp, hammer him to the floor until he begged for mercy.

That was the first and only time he and Corey fought. It hadn't been a pleasant thing. They were rather evenly matched in strength. But the surge of fury that took hold of Frazer that day had given him the edge. He'd eventually whipped Corey, beaten him into submission.

Several times Ella had tried to stop them. But there was no denying Frazer's towering black rage. He'd had his way. When it was all over he'd stalked out of the cabin, brushed aside Ella's restraining hands, gone to his horse, and ridden away.

He kept riding all that afternoon and most of the night. He wound up the next day in a small cow town on the other side of the Indian Head range. There he'd gone on a three-day drunk. No one knew him in the town and he did no talking. When he'd had enough he rode back to the Double-Y ranch. He gave no explanation of his absence to Margo Nash, nor had she asked him for any, but he guessed that she knew.

To friends and neighboring cowmen who inquired about his being away from the ranch, Frazer advanced the information that he'd gone north to inspect some blooded bulls he was thinking of buying for breeding purposes.

Corey had kept pretty much to himself and apparently no one in Two Forks realized anything had gone wrong or that Ella had switched affections. It was not until two weeks after his return that he met Corey in the foothills above the Double-Y ranch. He'd started to turn aside but Corey's quick call stopped him.

The marks of the conflict had completely disappeared from Corey's features. He rode close, for once looking very sober.

"I'm ten kinds of a skunk, Tom," he said, "I had it coming to me. If it would do any good I'd say have another go at me and I wouldn't lift a hand."

It was a considerable admission from Corey, who had his own sense of pride and a careless arrogance that overlooked, more often than not, the feelings and interests of others.

"There's nothing to talk about," Tom Frazer had said.

Corey grimaced. "I'd hoped in time you might forget. A man never had a better friend than you. Don't think I haven't always known that." He laughed. It was a strange, bitter laugh. "The funny part of it is that it was all for nothing."

Frazer remembered how he had stiffened to ask: "What do you mean?"

"Ella's getting married," Corey had said.

The pain, the agony had still been there deep inside Frazer when he answered. "All right. Congratulations."

"Hold on, Tom," Corey had said. "Not so fast. She's marrying Van Winston."

The shock of that announcement had hit Frazer right between the eyes. He'd thought, at first, that it was Corey's idea of a joke, and an unseemly one, at that. But the bitter, half-mocking light in Corey's eyes had told him it was true. And the reason for Ella's switch was rooted in her uncontrollable desire for security. She despaired of Corey's ever building his outfit into a paying ranch. She was afraid of his indolence, his inordinate liking for liquor and cards.

"In other words," Corey had concluded, "I've got no future."

"And Winston has," Frazer had added.

"Yeah. She knows what she wants—and Winston's got plenty of what she's always wanted and never had."

It was pretty cold-blooded. But Corey's bitterness hadn't lasted long. Perhaps his own feelings about Ella were not too deep. Even today Frazer wasn't entirely sure. Corey went his own mocking and sardonic way through life, apparently uncaring. Yet Frazer knew that he continued to see Ella secretly even after her engagement to Winston.

The fight between Frazer and Corey had, to all intents and purposes, been forgotten. Yet they never succeeded in regaining the easy and carefree camaraderie that had once marked their friendship. There was present now a constant feeling of strain.

Much of the strain was due to their flare-ups over Corey's association with Thorpe and the Big T crew. Frazer was not the only Two Forks cowman who believed that the Big T was a renegade outfit responsible for the rustling that was going on. Yet no one had ever caught a Big T rider with a stolen cow. Still, they were obviously a hard-case bunch. And it was Frazer's conviction that if a man ran with the wolves he soon became tagged with the name of a wolf. It didn't help Corey's reputation to be seen so frequently in the company of Thorpe. Frazer had sounded that warning on numerous occasions. But Corey didn't care what other people thought about his way of life.

The sure knowledge of Corey's failings—failings that made him so vulnerable to trouble—saddened Frazer. Now his own fiery temper had embroiled him in a fight with Pole Richmond. And that meant he'd have all of the Big T outfit on his neck. Richmond was not the kind of man to forget a hurt. Nor was Thorpe, for that matter. No man liked to be called a rustler to his face. Thorpe might not act immediately. But when the time was right he'd make his play to get back to his challenger. So Frazer realized he'd made another enemy. From now on he'd have to watch his back and ride with his gun loose in his holster.

The sight of Bassett's small ranch house pulled Frazer out of his somber mood of reflection. The weathered frame house lay in a small hollow surrounded by trees. He drifted into the yard, spotted a puncher over near the barn, and asked for Bassett.

Bassett had been there, the puncher told him, but had ridden out again to check a section of his north range. Frazer refused an invitation to get down and went on. A half mile from the ranch he struck the main road to Dunbar. He turned left, putting his back to the distant county seat, and rode toward home.

The road was a double-rutted ribbon of gray dust winding between thick stands of chaparral and now and then skirting a rocky bluff. As he pushed farther west, ridges and hills became more frequent. The ground turned shaly and hard and the yellow-tipped grass began to disappear. For the better part of half a mile the road ran under the shadow of a shaly bluff. Frazer kept his horse to a ground-eating canter until he struck a bend in the track.

At this point he never failed to stare up the long slope of the bluff, picking out the loose rock and dirt that reached up to the very top. A few rocks and brownish clumps of earth had spilled across the ruts from some minor slide. It was here that Ella's father had met his death several months ago. Speeding along the road in a buckboard, his mind half-numb from the whisky he had drunk in town, Jack Land had been trapped in one of the freak slides that occasionally inundated this section of the road. Land hadn't had a chance. The wagon had been smashed to kindling wood, the horse killed. Land himself had been buried alive in the avalanche.

It was still a dangerous spot. With the high, shaly bluff on one side and a deep culvert on the other side the road at this point was little more than a narrow gantlet between twin perils.

Frazer rode on quickly, leaving the road after another two miles to strike straight across country toward the Double-Y. Once again he traversed rolling grassland here and there dotted with clumps of brush.

Full dusk was draining the light out of the sky when he reached the Double-Y. He dismounted at the corral, stripped off his rig, hung the saddle on a peg in the barn, then draped the damp saddle blanket on the top pole of the corral.

Tex White and Hal Cooper were washing up at some basins set down on a bench behind the bunkhouse. They greeted him with grins and told him that Margo had gone off to see Polly Simmons at the Leaning S ranch and had not yet returned. Secretly Frazer was glad. He had parted with Margo under strained circumstances and he was not anxious to see her at the moment. Besides, he realized his face undoubtedly bore the marks of his fight with Pole Richmond and he wasn't in the mood to answer questions on the subject.

Tex White discovered that when he said to Frazer: "You have some trouble in town?"

Frazer ran a hand up and down the right side of his face. He felt a lumpy swelling under his eye. The edge of his jawbone was sore when he touched it. He looked at Tex White levelly and said: "Had a little run-in with Pole Richmond, that's all."

White waited for Frazer to elaborate, but the Double-Y ramrod offered no further information, and something in the hard set of Frazer's cheeks warned the puncher not to pursue the subject.

"Harry Yorke's gone up to the River Bend line shack to keep an eye on those Herefords," White informed Frazer. "You still want me to join him?"

"Yeah. First thing in the morning."

Frazer moved over to one of the basins and proceeded to wash the dust and grime off his hands and face. A little while later the cook yelled for them to come and get it and they went into the cook shack that adjoined the bunkhouse and sat down to a generous meal of fried steak, potatoes, stewed tomatoes, and jugs of coffee that was thick enough to cut with a knife.

Near the end of supper Frazer heard Margo ride in. She left her horse and riding gear at the corral and walked straight to the house. With supper finished, Frazer joined the hands in a game of penny-ante poker. He made no attempt to see Margo at the house. In fact, he hoped the cards would keep his mind off Margo and Ella and Corey. He had the distinct presentiment that Ella's marriage was going to end in trouble. And Corey—if he didn't keep away from Ella—would inevitably be caught in the violent aftermath.

The game didn't stop him from thinking. His mind kept wandering. Finally he threw in his cards and turned in.

He rose early the next morning, saw Tex White off to the River Bend line camp, then spent an hour in the breaking pen trying to take some kinks out of two half-wild broomtails from the hills. One of the horses, a roan, threw him twice. But he climbed back into the saddle a third time, with Hal Cooper lending a hand, and finally rode the stallion several times around the dust-fogged corral.

Feeling pleasurably weary after his exertions, he climbed through the bars of the corral. Cooper joined him, and they moved toward the well at the side of the ranch house. Both men halted halfway across the yard when they noted the fast-moving dust cloud two miles away along the crest of a ridge.

"Somebody is sure fogging it up," Cooper observed, shading his eyes with a brown, muscular hand.

Frazer squinted into the distance. "Coming this way," he said. "Looks like it might be Tex."

Suddenly a cold wind drilled up and down his spine. A premonition of disaster twisted the nerves in his chest into a tight knot. Only trouble would ride that fast on a horse.

Frazer and Cooper stood rooted in the yard watching the figure of that distant rider as it loomed larger and larger. There was a frozen rigidity about Frazer's features. His hands were knotted at his sides. He felt as if something deadly and unseen was closing in on him.

"It's Tex, all right," said Cooper after a moment. "I don't like it." The puncher took off his hat and rumpled his blond hair. He was a little drawn around the mouth.

The noise of the approaching horseman drew Margo onto the veranda. Frazer caught the flash of her white man's shirt tucked into blue levis and saw the way she paused at the top of the steps, but he didn't turn.

"Tom, that's Tex out there," she called. "He'll kill that horse he's riding. What's the matter?"

"Don't know," said Frazer gruffly. "But you can bet it isn't good."

He paced forward, going past the ranch house. Cooper went along. Margo came down the steps after them. White was leaning low over the mane of his laboring horse. He covered the last hundred yards in a terrific burst of speed. When he drew his foam-flecked horse to a halt the animal staggered and nearly went to its knees.

Cooper caught the bridle, steadied the weary horse. Frazer joined White, who half-fell out of the saddle and pitched against the Double-Y foreman. The young puncher, usually so cool and laconic, was thoroughly spent. But underneath the weariness that covered his face Frazer detected something else—fear and shock.

"Let's have it, Tex," he murmured. "You didn't ride that horse into the ground to bring us good news."

White's eyes lingered on Margo for an instant. She saw what he was thinking and said, "Whatever it is, you can say it in front of me."

"Harry Yorke is dead," he blurted suddenly.

Frazer experienced a lurching sensation in his stomach. He swung Tex White half around. "Do you know what you're saying?"

"Yeah, I know," said White dully. "I found him with a bullet hole right between the eyes."

Behind him Frazer heard Margo's shocked intake of breath. She pressed nearer. He saw the misery and hurt in her eyes. "Oh, my God," she said. "Poor Harry."

"What else?" demanded Frazer, anger beginning to replace the horror that had first taken hold of him.

"Those Herefords are gone. Every last one of them."

"We're done," moaned Cooper. "That licks us."

"Shut up!" Frazer ordered. "Just what did you find up there, Tex?"

Quickly White recounted how he had ridden up to the River Bend line camp. At first he'd been surprised to see Yorke's horse still cropping grass in the crude pole corral out behind the cabin. Then, as he drew nearer, he saw the scuffed, torn dirt in the yard indicating the recent presence of many riders.

Moving to the front of the cabin, he saw the barrel of a rifle protruding half out of the open window. He drew his Colt, gave a loud yell to announce his presence. Receiving no answer, he advanced on the cabin. When he reached the window he saw Yorke. The Double-Y puncher was sprawled on his side beneath the window. There was a blue-black hole in the middle of his forehead. Further investigation revealed that his body was cold. He had been dead for some time. The rustlers had caught him in the shack and picked him off, then lit out with the cattle.

"Which way did the cattle tracks go?" Frazer demanded.

"Northeast toward the river," White replied.

Frazer nodded. "Damn their souls," he said, his voice like a thin thread and sharp as the cutting blade of a knife. "They didn't wait long to make their move."

"What do you mean?" asked Margo.

He swung full around so that she had a clear look at his face. As her glance took in the bruises and discolorations on his cheeks he said, "The Big T. That's what I mean. I had a run-in with Pole Richmond yesterday in town and told Thorpe what I thought of him."

Margo's face registered sharp displeasure. "I'll bet Corey was involved." When Frazer didn't deny it, she went on: "I suppose he got in trouble and you had to pitch in."

"Richmond tried dealing a poker hand off the bottom of the deck."

"So you called him on it."

"Yeah. He had it coming."

"Maybe." Color was pushing up through the girl's cheeks. Her eyes were narrow, accusing slots. "Don't you think it's about time you stopped protecting Corey? He's not worth it."

Frazer turned away a moment to talk to Cooper. "Hal, saddle the bay team to the buckboard and beat it up to the camp. Bring Yorke's body back with you."

Cooper went off. White trudged away, too, heading for the well and a cool drink of water.

Margo waited for Frazer's attention to shuttle back to her. Then she asked through tight lips: "What are you planning to do?"

"First," he said grimly, "I'm going to see if I can pick up the trail of those Herefords. If the sign peters out at the river, as it did after the last raid, I figure on doing a little snooping around the Big T range."

"The Big T again!" Margo said, half in scorn. "Half the cowmen in Two Forks link Thorpe's name with the rustling. But nobody's ever been able to back the talk up with evidence. Think you can?"

"Thorpe's my man. I'll get him with the goods or die trying. One thing is certain. Between the rustling and Van Winston the Double-Y is in a tough spot."

Margo's brows drew together in a frown. "How does Winston figure in the picture?"

Frazer's voice dropped to a lower, regretful note. "I forgot to tell you. I stopped off at the bank yesterday afternoon. Ben Revere sold your note to Winston. Claims the bank needed cash."

Margo's eyes became singularly lifeless. Her eyes darted wildly about, as if seeking to flee from some nameless horror. She said out of the desperate sickness that gripped her: "That about winds up the Double-Y, doesn't it?" She couldn't keep the tremor out of her voice.

"Not yet," grated Frazer. "Winston and Thorpe are going to have a battle on their hands before they're finished."

"But we needed those cattle so much," Margo said. "We'll never pay off that note."

"There are still enough cows left on the Double-Y to sell."

"But if we sell them we'll have nothing left. We'll be bartering away our only chance of a good spring increase."

Frazer looked off toward the barn where Cooper was occupied with hitching the bays to the buckboard. He said slowly: "That note has a month to run yet. A lot can happen in that time. I'm not letting those Herefords go without a fight."

"If you back trail those cows take Hal or Tex with you," Margo said.

"No. One man on a trail job is better. Besides, they're needed here. We haven't any men to spare."

"But it's too dangerous to go alone," Margo insisted. There was a distinct shadow beneath her eyes. "Suppose you run into some of the Big T crew?"

Frazer's countenance remained hard and immobile. "I'll take that chance."

Margo came toward him. She lifted her face. A tendril of her silky hair touched his cheek. "I can't let you go," she said.

He grinned suddenly. "So you do care, after all."

He put his arms around her. The warmth of her lithe body set up an instant turmoil within him. She was all a man could ever want.

For a moment there was a yielding softness in her. Then she pushed away from him. "You presume too

65

much," she said in a voice not fully under control. "I—I just don't want you hurt."

A taciturn grimness thinned out Frazer's lips. Once again she had put him off, throwing up a wall between them. Her nearness was an agonizing thing. He said curtly: "Don't worry. It's a job to be done. I won't rest until I find those Herefords and get the men who killed Harry Yorke. If Thorpe's my man—and I reckon he is—he's going to learn that the Double-Y pays its debts."

He turned on his heel and tramped off toward the corral.

6   Frazer had no difficulty picking up the trail of the stolen Herefords. There was plenty of sign. From the number of horse tracks that mingled with the spoor of the cattle it was clear that the raiding party had been a large one.

Before taking the trail he had paused briefly to inspect the line shack. Harry Yorke lay beneath the cabin window just as Tex White had described. Death had laid a placid expression on the cowboy's face. His eyes were closed, his lips folded shut, and his body had the inertness that comes to men in sleep.

Frazer had to swallow a lump in his throat when he looked down at his puncher who had given his life for the Double-Y ranch. A deep feeling of remorse assailed him for having sent Yorke to the line camp alone. The puncher hadn't had a chance. True, he hadn't expected trouble of this nature. Yet he squirmed at the thought of how Yorke must have been fully aware of what he faced when the rustlers hit the cabin.

And Yorke had put up a fight. A half-dozen empty rifle shells scattered around the puncher's body testified to that. But somewhere out of the hostile night a heavy slug had entered the window with his name on it, and suddenly life was all over for him.

For a long moment Frazer lingered beside the corpse.

Sorrow was a sharp ache in him. Somehow he couldn't help feeling that he had sent Yorke to his doom. And the puncher's death went straight to the core of him, arousing a wild appetite for revenge. This was a rawhide land impelled by primitive passions. A man had to fight to survive, and Frazer resolved that somewhere on this range someone else would shortly die to balance the books for Harry Yorke.

Once on the trail of the rustled beef Frazer rode at a swift, steady trot. The land rolled and heaved in gentle swells of grassy hummocks and scattered bare knolls. It was fairly open going for five miles. Then brush and trees appeared with greater frequency and finally the hills grew steeper and rockier.

He crossed two purling creeks, the hoofmarks of cattle and horses sharply clear in the soft earth of the banks. But once the trail knifed into a wide granite gulch he knew he was entering the familiar stretch of malpais where presently all sign would peter out.

A torn bit of brush here and there, the main stem or root still white and fresh, told him he was still on the right track. But after the defile flattened out he found himself on a hard-rock plateau rising in gentle tiers to a wide granite bench. From the bench the trail dipped and wound down through a brush-filled coulee and on to another stretch of rocky terrain where there was absolutely no sign to be detected.

It was the old story. Frazer's countenance was darkly troubled. Dunbar River was just a half mile ahead. He spurred his roan gelding to a faster gait until he reached the stream. The ground sloped gradually down to the ford. At this point the river was scarcely a hundred yards wide and quite shallow. In the spring and fall, however, when the heavy rains came, a man had all he could do to swim his horse across.

Though the country within a few miles of the river was rough and barren, a number of willow trees bordered the stream on either side of the ford. It softened the harsh, bleak contours of the land.

The sun shone brightly down upon the smooth-flowing surface of the river and the reflection created a brassy glitter in Frazer's eyes. He pushed his roan gelding right down to the water, noting with the same bewilderment he had registered on his last quest for stolen cattle that where there should be hoofprints in the damp earth at the river's edge there was only the bare, unsullied ground.

He couldn't understand it. He was positive the cattle had been hazed straight toward the river. Yet if they had come this way unusual efforts must have been taken to obliterate the tracks.

Pausing just a moment to let the roan lower its head for a drink, Frazer splashed on through the shallow water to the far side. Here again in the damp earth he saw nothing that even hinted at the recent passage of a band of cattle and horsemen.

Patiently he scoured the far bank of the river for a distance of several hundred yards on either side of the ford. Then he cut inland, riding a great but narrowing circle, hoping to pick up some stray sign of prints. The effort proved futile.

Because he realized he was close to the southern extremities of Guy Thorpe's Big T range and because he was sure that somewhere in Thorpe's badlands domain could be found the answer to the riddle of the missing Herefords, he now cut back across the river and sent the roan along an old game trail that led away from the stream in a north-westerly direction.

In a short space of time he was winding through a stand of second-growth timber. Apparently a fire had raged through this section at one time, destroying many trees. Some blackened stumps were still in evidence. The trail detoured often to skirt deadfalls and scattered small boulders. Then after a while the trees thickened and he found himself climbing a steep slope. The way lay in full shadow with the leafy roof of the trees cutting off the slanting shafts of sunlight.

At the crest of the wooded ridge the trail drifted off to the west, leaving the pines behind. Ahead of him the country lay broken up into a long series of terraced ridges and scattered benches. He stopped for a few seconds to rest the roan. With eyes squinted to shut out the sun's white-hot glare, he studied the distant hills. Far off in a grassy basin he spotted a small herd of grazing cattle. They would be Big T critters. He saw no other signs of life. But as he was about to move on again he was attracted by a sudden glare over on an adjoining ridge. When he twisted around to regard the area more closely it had gone.

Pressure stirred his shoulder blades. It occurred to him the glare might have been caused by the sun striking a rifle barrel. There was no way of telling. However, he was in enemy country now, and if he ran into Pole Richmond or any other Big T punchers he could expect trouble.

He gigged the roan off the knoll and down into the protection of some rocks, all the while watching the yonder ridge. But there was nothing more to be seen. If a horseman was riding the ridge he was now keeping out of sight.

Frazer rode on, bearing west and north. Wherever he could, he kept to the trees. He was careful, too, to get off the ridges fast so that he would not be skylined for any great length of time.

Fifteen minutes of riding brought him to a little mesa. Once again he saw the grassy basin in which he had first seen some grazing cattle. The animals were not more than two miles away now. They appeared to be unguarded. Beyond them from the hollow between two hills came a faint tendril of gray smoke. That would be Big T headquarters.

Frazer had no definite plan in mind except to see if he could flush up some cows on Big T range wearing Double-Y brands or the recent scars of re-branding. He drifted past a low bench screened by brush. A scraping sound, almost like the scuff of a steel-shod shoe on rock, jerked him around in the saddle.

Simultaneously a sibilant murmur stirred the air above him. He darted a hand toward his gun and looked up. He was too late. A whirling lariat sped out of the chaparral. The noose settled over his shoulders, pinning his arms to his sides. He tried to wrench loose. But the rope was pulled taut.

"That's got him!" said a gruff voice he recognized as belonging to Pole Richmond.

The tall, somber-eyed Big T foreman pushed his light gray horse through the brush and trotted down off the bench. Another horse pushed through the screen. The rider was Ray Long. It was he who had roped Frazer. A third man, also mounted, appeared and joined Richmond. He was dark-haired and flat-faced and a stranger to Frazer.

Richmond said curtly to the dark-haired puncher: "Get his gun."

The man rode up behind the Double-Y ramrod and lifted the Colt from the holster and tossed it to Richmond. The latter stuck it in the waistband of his trousers.

"All right, loosen up on that rope, Ray," directed Richmond.

Long rode forward, the consequent slack in the rope permitting Frazer to free himself. He watched Long join the other two Big T men, then took a slow, deliberate look at Richmond's bruised features. He knew he was in bad trouble. The dull, opaque glare of Richmond's eyes and the savage twisting of his torn lips told him that. The sunlit air was still and oppressive with the feeling of raw passions lightly held in check.

Frazer's feelings were rioting within him. There were carved lines around his eyes that hadn't been there a moment before. But he said with reckless hard care: "Pole, you look as if someone ran your face through a meat grinder."

Rage climbed hotly through the Big T foreman. The fingers of his right hand grew white and hard around the cedar butt of his Colt. "When I get through with you, Frazer," he growled, "you're going to be bait for the buzzards."

"Are you sure you've got enough help?" Frazer asked. "There are only three of you."

A meager smile tugged at Frazer's mouth. There was no mirth in it and no humor, only a wicked mockery.

"You won't be smiling when I've finished," Richmond told him. "But first I want to know what you're doing on Big T range."

"Looking for stolen Double-Y beef," Frazer replied promptly.

"You're in the wrong place."

"I'm not so sure of that." There was a pale, warning glow in Frazer's blue eyes. "Somebody raided our River Bend line camp last night, got away with a hundred Herefords, and killed Harry Yorke."

Richmond's upper lip curled. He said flatly: "That's too bad. What do you want me to do about it?"

"I don't know—yet," said Frazer. "I've an idea you could tell me about those cows and about Yorke too."

"You're loco!" snarled Richmond.

"Maybe." Frazer sat his horse stiffly. He was watching the barrel of Richmond's gun and he saw that Long and the other Big T puncher were on the alert, ready to burn

72

powder if the need arose. Then he added savagely: "But if I ever find out that a Big T bullet killed Yorke, I'm coming after you and Thorpe and I'll come with a smoking six."

Hot blood was pumping into Frazer's head. He strained forward, every muscle tense. There was cold defiance in every inch of his whip-steel frame. Richmond and the others saw it and grew wary. Richmond's gun steadied on Frazer's chest.

"You're all through calling the Big T a rustling outfit," he said. "I'm going to take you apart piece by piece." Richmond gestured imperiously with the gun. "Climb down."

Suddenly death was an actual smell in the hot, dry atmosphere. Looking at Richmond, Frazer understood at once that Richmond had no intention of making this a fair fight. Richmond was too far gone in fury. Destructive impulses were warping his brain. This was his chance for revenge and he meant to make the most of it. And Frazer knew that whatever Richmond did, it would not be pretty. The cold certainty of that honed Frazer's senses to a fine, wire-tight edge.

"Get down!" Richmond repeated, his voice thick with passion.

In the dread silence that followed this second command Frazer felt evil pressing around him like a miasmic fog. Then with a fatalistic rashness he flung himself at Richmond. One arm batted down the Big T foreman's upswinging gun hand. Frazer heard the roar of a shot as Richmond squeezed the trigger. Then he clubbed Richmond alongside the head with a solid right. Richmond's horse spooked up and leaped forward. The renegade lost his seat and the force of Frazer's lunge carried them out of the saddle. They struck the earth with a solid thump.

Frazer heard Ray Long's angry shout and knew the Big

T puncher would be piling off his pony to join the fray. Richmond drove a knee into Frazer's groin. Swift torture knotted all the nerves in his belly. He pounded Richmond with a left and right, started to wrench away. Then a gun barrel descended on the side of his head. A crazy pattern of colored lights spun before Frazer's eyes. Dazed and numbed, he struggled to get to his knees. Long and the other man got around behind him, grabbed his arms, and hauled him to his feet.

"Hold him like that!" ordered Pole Richmond. He picked himself up off the ground. There was a fresh cut on his lip. Blood seeped from it. He wiped it away with the back of his hand.

"How do you feel, Pole?" Frazer asked. One of his solid rights had caught the ramrod's puffed eye and he knew the man was in pain.

"You won't be able to feel when I'm finished with you," said Richmond, and smashed a left to the side of Frazer's face.

Frazer tried to twist away from Long and his companion. But each man had a grip on an arm and they held him firm. He looked at Richmond through metal-bright eyes. Richmond was moving in again, his right fist cocked for another swing.

"So that's how it's going to be," Frazer murmured. A dull inner pressure squeezed him. He felt as if the jaws of a vise were slowly contracting around his chest.

Richmond swung again. Frazer saw it coming and jerked away, dragging his captors with him. The blow missed.

"Hold him still, you fools!" Richmond raged. To Frazer he said: "Now we'll see how tough you are!"

He moved in close. His right arm flashed again. Once more Frazer tried to elude the punch. But the two Big T punchers held him rigid. The best he could do was shift

74

his head so the blow grazed his face. But he couldn't avoid the flurry of fists that Richmond poured into him after that. They came with lightning rapidity, hard, shocking blows that shook him and dazed him.

A slashing left hook split Frazer's lower lip. A chopping right cut a gash over his left eye. Wickedly Richmond concentrated on the injured optic. Blow after blow struck the gash, widening it and spilling blood down Frazer's face. He grew numb and dizzy. Water seemed to be flowing through his legs instead of blood.

"How do you like that, friend?" grated Richmond as he paused for breath. A malevolent gleam lit up his dark eyes. The depth of his exertions had accelerated his breathing. He pushed his face close to Frazer, relishing the carnage he had already wrought upon Frazer's features and anticipating further unholy pleasures to come.

Despite the pain that was consuming him Frazer showed no break in his hard, unruffled front. "I don't think much of you as a butcher, Pole," he muttered. "You'll have to do better."

Frazer's taunt drove Richmond to a frenzy. Again he rushed in and peppered the Double-Y ramrod with slogging blows. Frazer's eye was swelling now. The lid was drawn almost shut. A sharp left brought a puffy lump of fiery tissue into view beneath the other eye. His lip was cut in two more places. Blood filled his mouth.

Frazer struggled feebly, still trying to get free so he could lash out at Richmond. But Long and the other puncher held him firm. And now he no longer had the strength to turn his head or rock with the blows. They came in a steady, maddening rhythm. A growing numbness spread over Frazer's brain. His head seemed to be like a bouncing ball. It was never still. It rocked and lurched on the wide pivot of his neck. It was huge too. It felt like two or three heads.

He no longer could see clearly. Richmond's image kept weaving in front of his pain-misted gaze. Richmond's pumping fists were nothing but a reddish blur. Frazer sagged, his knees buckling and pulling his two captors forward. Cruelly they jerked him upright again, holding him as a target for another crushing right to the face.

"Have you had enough, Frazer?"

Richmond's voice seemed far away. It had a disembodied quality. His wickedly smiling face was going around in circles. Then the face vanished in a dark, churning curtain shot through with ruddy sparks.

The feeble flicker of life still in Frazer rebelled. Richmond was waiting for him to crawl. He wanted him to beg for mercy. But there was too much iron in Frazer ever to give in. Though he was stricken and badly hurt, he was still unrelenting. Not Richmond nor any man could break Frazer to his will.

It took a tremendous effort to form the words of a reply. But Frazer managed it. "Keep on, Pole," he said. His voice was little more than a whisper. "You're not man enough to finish the job."

Richmond cursed. A long, gasping breath spilled from his lungs. He came at Frazer once more. His arms were weary. But hate was still a corroding flux in his veins. He hit Frazer with a left and a right, putting every ounce of strength into the blows. They struck home. Frazer hardly felt the bone-thudding impact of Richmond's knuckles. His legs buckled again and suddenly he was falling down and down into a bottomless black void.

7   Margo was puttering around the small flower garden on the west side of the Double-Y ranch house when she first heard the sound of a horse approaching. Leaning on the trowel with which she had been working in the dry earth, she looked out across the flats.

A horse was coming along at a slow trot, headed straight for the ranch. At first Margo thought the animal was riderless. Then she saw that the rider was sprawled forward with his face buried in the animal's mane. The sight pulled Margo to her feet. It was then that a closer glance showed her that the horse was a roan. She swayed to a sickening lurch of fear as she recognized Frazer's favorite saddler.

The trowel dropped unheeded from her fingers. Fear brought a hard lump into her throat. She gasped for breath. She took a few stumbling steps across the yard. The roan came on at a tired trot, bringing into full view the ragdoll figure of Tom Frazer lashed to his saddle with rope.

An icy hand seemed to encircle Margo's heart as she lunged forward to intercept the roan gelding. She couldn't even run. Her legs seemed to be fashioned of rubber. They quivered uncontrollably. It was a struggle to remain on her feet.

The roan started to swing past the veranda. Margo broke her uneven stride. She leaped for the bridle. By a stroke of luck she caught it in her hand and dragged the horse to a stop. She moved past the roan's head, put her fingers on Frazer's shoulder.

Somehow the pressure of Margo's touch or the sudden cessation of movement penetrated the black veil of unconsciousness. Frazer lifted his head, his bruised face turning toward her. Margo got one look at the swollen mass of flesh and bone that had been Frazer's face and screamed in horror. All that she could see of his eyes were vacant, staring slits almost lost in purplish mounds of battered skin tissue. It was the face of a stranger—a grotesque, frightening travesty, a hideous mask that had no relation to reality.

"Oh, Tom—my dear!" she cried. "What have they done to you?"

Frazer didn't hear her. His slitted eyes were glazed. Even while tears stung Margo's eyelids and horror churned in her like a wooden spoon stirring her insides Frazer slumped face forward again into the roan's silky, flowing mane.

"Tex! Tex!" she called at the top of her voice. "Come here! Hurry! It's Tom. He's hurt."

Tex White came at a dead run from behind the barn. He saw Margo up close against the roan, slashing at the ropes that held Frazer to the saddle.

"Wait, Margo!" he said. "Let me handle this."

Dust sprang up from his skidding boots when he reached Margo.

"Is he shot?" he asked.

"I—I don't know," Margo said. Her eyes were shiny wet and she couldn't keep the tremble out of her lips. "But he's hurt—bad."

White took the knife from the girl's hand and quickly

severed the ropes that bound Frazer's legs together around the roan's belly. Then he cut the thin rope that had kept his arms locked around the saddler's neck.

Immediately Frazer's body started to slide out of the kack. White caught him. Even at that the Double-Y foreman's weight almost bore the young puncher to the ground. As he heaved Frazer up and over his shoulder he noticed Frazer's battered features. "My God—his face!" he exclaimed. "Looks like—like a horse stomped him."

"Hurry!" Margo cried. "Get him inside."

White shouldered Frazer's limp body and staggered toward the house. Margo helped him up the veranda steps.

"The front room—on the couch in there," she said, holding open the door so White could pass through with his burden.

The puncher slammed against the deal table in the room's center, almost upending it. But he reached the couch without further mishap and deposited Frazer on it. The Double-Y ramrod didn't move. Margo, her cheeks putty-colored, her eyes showing white, startled rims, fell to her knees beside the couch and placed her hand on Frazer's chest.

"Margo—he—he isn't dead?" White asked fearfully.

The girl raised her curly-haired head after a moment. "No—no," she said. "But I—I'm afraid. His face—it looks so——" She broke off in panic. "Tex, you've got to ride to town for the doctor. Find him—wherever he is."

Margo's smooth ivory skin was drawn tightly over her cheekbones. She looked gaunt and haggard. Panic was a cold tide dashing its brutal waves against her, drowning her in a dark well of dread.

"But you—will you be all right, Margo?" White asked.

"Go!" she cried. "Don't worry about me. It's Tom. He—he may be dying." She pushed against him with the

79

flat of her hands. She saw the righteous anger in his face and she saw, also, the questions that were rising to his lips. "Go on, Tex!" she insisted. "And ride like you've never ridden before!"

White turned and dashed from the room. Margo went back to the couch. Frazer lay as still as death. Tears sprang to her eyes again when she saw how cruelly torn and lacerated his features were. It would be an hour or more before White could return with the doctor. In that time anything could happen.

The terrible thought chilled Margo to the core of her being. She had to do something so she rushed into the kitchen and put some water on the stove to boil. Then she kept running back and forth between the rooms, hoping to see some stir of life in Frazer, while she waited for the water to become hot.

When at last it was hot she got some clean cloths and began to bathe his face, wiping the blood and grime from it. She was very gentle, but her hands kept shaking, and the cold feeling of horror would not leave her.

Afterward, she got some brandy and tried to force a little of the liquid into Frazer's mouth. But he was completely lax and inert. Though she got some of the brandy past his lips, it trickled out again and slid down his chin. She gave up and sank into a chair that she had pulled up beside the couch.

Never in all her days had she seen anyone's face as bruised and swollen as Frazer's. She wondered what had happened during his ride into the badlands. Had he run into some of Guy Thorpe's crew? That seemed to be the only answer. The fact that he was still alive was a miracle.

She had to force herself to look at his face. It was an altogether unnerving sight. Suddenly she was filled with an unutterable sadness and despair. She remembered now how big and strong and capable he had always been. He had been a rock to lean upon. There had always been something indestructible and invulnerable about him. He was a man utterly without fear—a man who could be depended on to come through any trial or danger with colors flying.

That was the picture of Tom Frazer Margo had always carried with her. Now, seeing him broken and battered, she was completely unnerved. She felt her own little world tumbling down around her. It was like a bitter foretaste of ruin. For Tom Frazer was the Double-Y. Without him nothing could save the ranch.

Only now did Margo admit the depth of her feeling for him. Only now did she realize that the Double-Y was valueless to her unless Tom was there. She wanted him so much that she was all one ache inside. She gazed at him, so still and immobile, with a longing and a hunger that were undisguised. And she kept on looking at him as if by the very power of her longing she might rouse him to consciousness.

She leaned close, watching the faint rise and fall of his chest that indicated life was still in him. She would have kissed him if she hadn't been afraid of hurting his smashed lips.

The minutes dragged on with agonizing slowness. There was a hollow emptiness in Margo. Her throat burned with a choking pain. She knew it was from the tears that welled up in her, demanding release.

A dozen times she rose to walk to the window and stare across the prairie, seeking the dust cloud that would announce the approach of Tex White and the doctor. But the prairie remained empty.

At last, after what seemed an eternity of waiting, Margo saw the dust cloud she was seeking. Her heart began hammering in a surge of renewed hope. She was waiting at the door when Tex White and Dr. Fred Marlow slid from their horses at the foot of the veranda steps.

"Hurry, Dr. Marlow," Margo urged. "Tom is still unconscious. He—he hasn't even moved."

Marlow, a middle-aged man with prematurely gray hair and bushy gray eyebrows in a tired, fleshy face, came up the steps with his black bag. He patted Margo's arm reassuringly as he pushed past her into the room where Frazer lay.

Accustomed as Marlow was to violence and death in all forms, he drew a rasping breath when he sighted the Double-Y ramrod's beaten face. "My God, Margo!" he exclaimed. "How did this happen? Tom's in terrible shape."

"He went after some stolen Herefords," Margo said woodenly. "He told me he expected to hit for Dunbar River and if he lost the trail to do some looking around on Big T range."

The doctor frowned. His brown eyes grew somber. "Thd old story. Guy Thorpe again. Did Tom dig up any evidence to show that Thorpe was behind the raid?"

"No."

"I can damn well guess how he got that face, though," put in Tex White angrily. "He had a fight with Pole Richard yesterday and beat him up. I'm betting Tom ran into some of the Big T buckaroos and they decided to bust him up."

Marlow set his bag down on a chair, opened it up, and removed a stethoscope. He said: "A bullet would have been easier on him."

White replied grimly: "Yeah. I reckon the Big T bunch figured the same so they beat him."

The doctor turned away to examine Frazer, and an uneasy silence fell upon the room. Marlow spent a good deal of time on Frazer's facial bruises, then transferred his attention to his skull. He worked with a swift and careful precision. He said nothing, and Margo was too unnerved to venture any questions.

Finally the doctor stripped Frazer to the waist and began probing with gentle, sensitive fingers for internal injuries. When he finished he placed his stethoscope back in his bag, then brought out a few small envelopes filled with a whitish powder.

"Is—is he going to be all right?" Margo queried.

"Yes, Margo," he said. "He's been through something, though. He's had no internal injuries. I can see no breaks in the bones of the face and there's no skull fracture."

Margo gripped Marlow's arm. Her voice leaped at him. "But why hasn't he regained consciousness?"

"From what I can see," the doctor told her, "he's got a slight concussion. Rest will fix that. He should be coming around soon now. Now if you have some brandy——"

"Right here," Margo interrupted, going to the table where she had deposited the bottle and glass.

Marlow took them from her. He uncorked the bottle, poured some brandy in a glass. Then he went to the couch, put an arm beneath Frazer's shoulders, raised him slightly, and forced some of the dark liquid down the ramrod's throat. There was no immediate reaction. Then Marlow asked for some water. Margo brought a glass full. The doctor spilled some powder from one of the little envelopes into the water and forced a good portion of that into Frazer.

After that he removed the support of his arm from Frazer's shoulders and took a jar of salve from his bag.

"You can spread some of this salve on a wet cloth," he told Margo. "Make a poultice of it and keep it on his face. It'll help to take the swelling down." He passed a few envelopes of powder to the girl. "And give him one of these powders in a half glass of water every four hours. That's all. I'll stop by tomorrow again."

Margo listened carefully, her lips ridged with an odd intentness. "You're sure he'll be all right?" she demanded.

"Take my word for it, Margo," the doctor said, "in a week he'll be back to normal though it'll take a spell longer than that for all the bruises to heal completely."

Marlow closed his bag and went out. At a signal from Margo Tex White also left the room. She walked to the door, watched the doctor ride off toward town, then resumed her seat beside the couch. She meant to keep a constant vigil beside Frazer until he came to.

Once again as she looked at him she felt numb and frightened. He seemed so helpless and alone. Somehow the very bigness of him made his present condition more abject and shattering.

There was no change for fifteen minutes. Only the slow rise and fall of Frazer's chest indicated that life still pulsed in his veins. Then Margo noticed an influx of color in his cheeks. It was a gradual process, at first almost un-noticeable. Immediately Margo's feelings began to soar. She rose and bent close to Frazer.

A pang of pity stabbed her when she noted the ugly reds and purples of his crushed skin. His lips were swollen and cracked. Tenderness welled up in her, and she brought her soft, trembling mouth against his. It was a light, feathery kiss. But as Margo drew away Frazer's body stirred. His eyelids squeezed open. Margo was so startled she almost fell back in the chair.

"Margo!" Frazer's lips moved in a hoarse, choking whisper.

She dropped to her knees beside the couch and took one of Frazer's hands in hers. "I've been so afraid you'd never open your eyes again."

"It's good—to—have you here," Frazer murmured brokenly.

Margo's eyes misted with hot tears. A long sigh came

out of her. "Tom—your face! It—it must have been terrible."

The back of Frazer's head ached. There was a steady, throbbing pain in his cheeks and in the swollen puffs of flesh around his eyes. But he forgot the pain in the magic of Margo's nearness.

"I—I seem to remember you—kissing me," he said.

Margo reddened. Frazer tried to smile. But the effort sent a cruel stab of agony through the muscles around his mouth. Margo's answer, delayed and hesitant, came at last. "Yes, Tom. I—I did kiss you."

The torn slits that were Frazer's eyes lingered on Margo's face. He studied her with curious intentness, as if he planned to memorize all the details of her features lest he never see her again. There was sweetness in her and a richness that could last a man to the end of his days. Shadow made deep pools in her eyes. Her lips were gently curving and made for the ritual of loving. He knew deep in his heart that he would do anything to have Margo, and looked intently for a sign that the same eager fires churned in her own blood.

"Did you mean it?" he said.

"Maybe," she replied in a summer-soft tone.

Then her breath was upon his cheek and she fell against him, her arms going around him. Frazer felt the wild, frenzied beating of her heart. His own feelings were in a tumult. Having Margo in his arms was well worth any pain, no matter how severe.

After a moment he was conscious of the fact that she was sobbing. She was trembling, too, and he tightened his arm around her. "Margo, Margo," he said. "It's—it's all right."

She lifted her tear-streaked face and said in a choking voice, "I am a baby. But—but seeing you so beaten, Tom. I—I just couldn't help it."

"Knowing you care makes it that much easier," he said.

Margo wiped her eyes with a handkerchief, then kissed his lips lightly again. Turning to the table, she noted the jar of salve. "Dr. Marlow was here," she said. "He told me to make a poultice with some of that salve to bring down the swelling." She started to move away.

He pulled her down beside him again. "Wait. First, tell me how I got here. I remember going down. The rest is just a blank."

Quickly Margo told how the roan had trotted into the ranch yard with his body lashed to the saddle in an upright position.

Frazer's eyes hardened. "They went to a lot of trouble."

Margo's attention quickened. "Who was it? Thorpe's crowd?"

Frazer's head moved in a gesture of assent. "I ran into Pole Richmond, Ray Long, and another man on Big T range after losing the trail of those Herefords up around the Dunbar River ford." Then in slow, precise phrases he gave a brief account of the beating he had received.

When he had finished Margo sat very still. Horror washed whitely across her cheeks. "You mean Long and the other man held you while Richmond kept hitting you?" she asked.

"Yeah."

"Oh, my dear," Margo said, "that must have been terrible."

Again Frazer tried to smile. But the effort cost too much in pain. He lifted a hand to his swollen face, let his fingers trace the bruised skin. "Do you have a mirror, Margo?" he asked.

She nodded and rose. Going to the next room, she came back with a small wall mirror and held it above the couch so Frazer could stare at his own reflection.

The sight of his own face was as much of a shock to Frazer as it had first been to Margo. He turned altogether still. Cold lights flickered in his slitted blue eyes. "They really did a job on me," he said in a voice roughened by rage.

"Tom, you shouldn't have gone up there alone," Margo told him.

"I'd do it again," he said, his iron will showing through his talk.

Margo's face became tinged with sadness and fear. "Now you'll be wanting to get even with Richmond," she said.

"I've got time," he told her.

She said with sharp vehemence, "No, Tom. There's no good in it. After you've recovered you'd better go away."

"And leave you here to face the music?"

"You expect more trouble?"

"This is only the beginning," Frazer told her grimly. "We've got Winston on one side of us holding that note and Thorpe on the other side rustling Double-Y beef. Between them they'll put the squeeze on us. I aim to stop them if I can."

Margo's face was pale now. Little beads of perspiration showed on her tanned forehead. "But what can you do?"

"I don't know—yet. But I know this: I've only begun to fight." Frazer's long, muscular body shook with the violence of his feelings. "Richmond is going to be sorry he didn't finish me."

Frazer's words thrilled Margo even as they filled her with renewed fear. Already he was a marked man on the range. Wherever he went Big T men would be gunning for him. And she had a positive conviction that the next time the Big T and the Double-Y clashed it would be over smoking guns. Harry Yorke was dead, possibly at Big T hands. And Tom was horribly beaten. That left

Tex White, Hal Cooper, and herself. Two men and a girl in a knockdown fight for survival.

"Tom," Margo said, "I'd rather give up now than risk more killing. It's not worth it."

"No!" he said. "I won't let you give up. While we've still got cows on Double-Y grass and three men to ride the hills we'll fight."

"But there are only Tex and Hal. You can't ride now."

"I'll be back in the saddle before the end of the week," Frazer told her, his hands clenching into hard-knuckled fists.

8   Three days after the beating Frazer was permitted to get out of bed. He had fretted so much at being confined to the ranch house that Marlow had finally sanctioned his sitting in a chair on the veranda. The swelling had gone down considerably and some of the soreness was disappearing from the bruised tissues. As far as he was concerned, he felt ready to ride again. But the doctor had counseled a few more days of rest. Frazer agreed, though not with good grace.

Even sitting on a chair outside made him feel cramped. The sight of Hal Cooper and Tex White riding out on range chores filled him with a restlessness he found difficult to control.

He had gotten up and was pacing slowly up and down the veranda when Sheriff Fred Landon pulled in from town. Landon was a thin, wiry man, medium tall and bowlegged from long hours spent in the saddle. Crow's-foot wrinkles made deep tracks around his gray eyes. His cheeks were sunken, his face long and narrow, tapering to a pointed chin.

Frazer was happy to see him and came to the head of the steps to greet the lawman. "Howdy, Fred. What brings you out here?"

"Heard in town you've had some trouble," Landon murmured in a dry voice. He peered shrewdly at Frazer's face. "Seems like something else has been going on nobody told me about. Who stepped on your face?"

Frazer ignored the question. He said, "Wish you'd been here four days ago. We lost a big herd of Herefords and somebody got Harry Yorke."

Landon shook his head. His gaunt cheeks pinched inward. "I'm sorry about that, Tom," he said. "I've been busy up in Dunbar on a stagecoach robbery. Just pulled into Two Forks this morning. Got any ideas about the rustling or Yorke's shooting?"

"The same old cry," Frazer told him.

"Thorpe again?"

"Yeah, but no evidence to pin it on him."

A sultry irritation rolled through the sheriff. "By God, this country is getting too big for one man to handle. Wish I had a couple of good deputies" He stopped. Again he peered at Frazer's bruised features. "Heard you had a ruckus with Pole Richmond in town. That face of yours got anything to do with it?"

"Plenty," replied Frazer, and repeated his experiences which had culminated in the beating.

"Damn that Richmond," muttered Landon. "Must be some Indian in him. You fixing to prefer charges against him?"

"Fred, you know me better than that," Frazer retorted, drawing himself together like a coiled spring.

"Reckon I do, Tom." The sheriff's attention lingered on the puffy swellings under Frazer's steel-blue eyes. "You're lucky they didn't drill you full of slugs."

Frazer's mouth was a tight trap. He said flatly, "That's where Richmond made a mistake. There'll be a different story to tell the next time I see him."

"Watch yourself," Landon warned. He looked suddenly tired and worn and old. The responsibilities of his office weighed heavily on his narrow shoulders. He was just one man in a job that was too big for him. The sound of Margo moving about somewhere inside the house drew his thin brows into a frown. "I'd like to get that beef back for Margo. How'd you like to be a deputy, Tom?"

"Nothing doing. I don't want to be tied down by any legal strings. There's more trouble coming. I feel it in my bones. A deputy's star would only get in my way."

Landon's sun-browned features showed neither surprise nor disappointment. "Too bad," he said. "I sure could use you. Reckon I'll take a *pasear* up in the hills and see if I can pick up anything."

"It's a cold trail, Fred," Frazer informed him. "And you'll find all sign gone by the time you hit the river ford."

Landon's lips set stubbornly. "I'll have a look anyhow. So long."

"So long, Fred," Frazer said, and watched him go back to his horse, mount, and swing off at a fast lope toward the hills.

Frazer started down the steps. He couldn't tolerate the enforced idleness. He would ride and get some of the kinks out of his system. Halfway across the yard Margo hailed him.

"Tom, where are you going?" She had emerged from the house and was standing on the veranda.

"Just for a ride."

Margo's face stiffened in quick concern. She hurried down the steps and walked up to him. "Tom," she said tensely, "you're not thinking of doing anything crazy, are you?"

"You mean Pole Richmond?" he queried.

"Yes. You mustn't go to the Big T."

"I'm not ready yet, Margo," he said. "I've got to move around a little. Sticking by the ranch gets on my nerves."

"Be careful, please," she begged.

"Sure."

Sunlight picked up tiny golden glints in Margo's hair. She was close to him, and her warm loveliness was a strong call to Frazer's aroused senses. He pulled her against him, kissing her roughly though the pressure of her lips sent a stab of pain through him. He felt her yield to him, felt her mouth come alive. Then she stiffened. He dropped his arms. There was a sudden constraint in her manner.

"Maybe I shouldn't have done that," he said.

She looked fully at him. For one brief instant he saw deeply into her eyes. A bright flame burned there, a tempest of feeling. It unsettled him at the same time that it filled him with a wild, straining hope. She had been strangely reserved with him the last few days. Now the passion he saw reflected in her eyes made his blood race.

But as suddenly as the flame appeared it vanished and an odd shyness came over her. "I—I've got to get used—to us," she said. She had let herself go and she wasn't quite ready. The tumult of her own rash feelings frightened her.

Frazer said roughly, in embarrassment, "I'll be back in a little while," and hurried away from her, going to the corral.

He roped his favorite roan, tossed on a rig, and climbed aboard. He waved to Margo as he rode by. The feel of a horse under his legs was a tonic to him. The warm sun was good too. For a little while the sheer exhilaration of riding blotted out all other thoughts. The ache in the back of his head was gone and the jarring gait of the roan did not bother him.

With nothing special to do he headed for Bill Corey's spread. He wondered why Corey had not been over to see him. They usually saw each other a few times each week. Of course Corey had no way of knowing about the fight up in the hills. The Big T had obviously done no talking about it or the sheriff would have heard the story in town.

When he reached Corey's ranch he found the place deserted. There was a layer of dust on the kitchen table where Corey usually had his meals when at home. From appearances it looked as if Corey had not been around in several days. His absence puzzled Frazer.

He rode on, making a short circuit through the lower foothills before swinging back to the Double-Y outfit.

At ten the next morning the sheriff reappeared. His long, thin face was morose and unhappy. He had made a dry camp in the hills during the night. He had spent most of the previous day in the saddle, hunting for the stolen Double-Y cattle. But he had met with failure.

"It's got me beat," he said, "where those cows could have gone."

"I'll find out," Frazer told him grimly, "if I have to spend all my nights in the saddle."

"What do you mean?"

"The rustlers aren't finished yet. We've still got cows left. I aim to night-hawk one of our remaining herds and be on hand when the next raid is pulled."

The sheriff looked doubtful. "It's a long chance. I wish you luck. If you need me, I'll be in Two Forks for the next few days."

He lifted his reins and trotted wearily out of the yard.

An hour later, while Frazer was preparing to enter the corral to rope out a horse for himself, Bill Corey rode in.

"My God, Tom, what happened to your face?" he said as Frazer turned from the corral to greet him.

"You should have seen it three days ago," Frazer told him, and once again gave an account of his run-in with Pole Richmond.

"The damned sidewinder!" Corey raged. "Killing is too good for him." And deep inside Corey a hollow, accusing

93

voice whispered: What are you talking about? You know all about it. Haven't you been with Richmond and the Big T crew driving a bunch of rebranded Double-Y cows from last month's rustling job over the state line? There's your best friend beaten up by the sneaking hard cases you ride with.

The accusing voice had been nagging Corey more than usual lately. He had his moments of savage self-abasement when he felt miserable and ashamed at the way he made his living. He hadn't any right to the friendship of a man like Tom Frazer. Every time he rode with Thorpe's owl hooters he betrayed Frazer or one of his other neighbors. He had gone steadily down the ladder these last few months. The rustling was bad enough. But when Harry Yorke was killed he had been engulfed by a terrible nausea. That was something he hadn't counted on—something he wanted no part of.

And now they'd hit directly at Tom. There were still enough discolorations and bruises on Frazer's face to tell Corey what a hideous experience that must have been. And he'd had to listen to Richmond tell Thorpe about it, conscious all the while that Richmond was relishing the story all the more because he knew it would burn him—Corey—up.

Anger stormed wildly through Corey. The beating had been much worse than he imagined it. It would be months before Frazer's face healed up completely. Some of the scars he would carry with him for the rest of his life. The thought was maddening. It was like a knife rending his insides. Richmond had a killing coming to him.

"Kid, I wish I'd been with you," Corey murmured. "It might have been a different story."

"Where were you?" Frazer asked. "I rode over to your place yesterday. Nobody was around. Looked like you hadn't been there for days."

A shadowed wariness pulled a film across Corey's eyes. He spoke sharply. "I spent a couple of days up in Ardmore, across the Indian Heads, trying to buy some blooded bulls."

Surprise honed the lines of Frazer's craggy face to a thinner edge. "Didn't know you had the money to invest in blooded stock," he said.

Corey colored. Lying wasn't easy for him. "My poker luck finally changed the other night."

Frazer grinned. "You never get enough, do you, Bill?" The grin faded and Frazer asked: "How many bulls did you buy?"

"None." Corey sounded abrupt. "Didn't see any decent stock." He picked up the reins which had lain slack along his pony's mane. The direction of their conversation didn't please him. It was bad enough that the sight of Frazer's battered face filled him with a sickening feeling of self-reproach. He kept blaming himself for what had happened. If he stayed any longer he'd be spilling his insides to Frazer. "Well," he added, "got to get back home. Don't forget. If you need me, I'll be around."

"Sure, Bill, and thanks."

Frazer, a little puzzled and hurt by Corey's hurried departure, turned back to the corral. A somber sadness hit him. The old free-and-easy days were gone. Trouble was on the land. It quivered in the air like a muted sound of distant drums. And the friendship that had once brought Corey and himself closely together was coming apart at the seams. They were no longer at ease with each other. A good thing had turned sour.

9   Corey did not go home. Sticking to the wagon road until a wooded ridge hid him from the view of any watchers at the Double-Y ranch, he spurred his big-muscled piebald horse into a twisting game trail that struck off into a stretch of heavy timber.

He rode steadily for twenty minutes, keeping off the ridges and staying in the protection of trees whenever the vagaries of the trail permitted. The country rose in gradual folds before him, angling higher and higher. The piebald knew its way without guidance, leaving one trail for another, now clattering through a high-walled canyon, now trotting briskly across scattered high mesas.

Finally at a point not more than three miles south of the Dunbar River ford Corey spurred out of a patch of trees into a clearing. A small weathered line cabin jutted against a rocky twenty-foot bluff. It looked run-down and deserted. Corey's eyes lit up in expectancy. He rode on, scanning the brush off to his left. He caught sight of a ground-tied pony and immediately smiled.

The cabin had once been used as a line shack by Margo's father in the days when the Double-Y had run big herds of cattle. Now it was abandoned. A lean-to barn in the rear had been blown down in a high wind. The fallen boards were piled in a jumbled heap, rotting under the hot sun.

Corey drew the piebald to a halt at the side of the cabin and dismounted. As he walked around to the front the door opened and Ella came forward.

"Where have you been?" she asked petulantly.

"What kind of a greeting do you call that?" Corey demanded. He swaggered up to her and hauled her against his chest with a wide sweep of his arms.

Ella fought him for an instant, then pulled his head down in a sudden fierce gesture and kissed him. It was a very thorough kiss. They remained locked in each other's arms for a long time. Ella's nails dug into the back of Corey's neck. When he finally released her there was an aroused shine in Ella's eyes.

"Bill, do you realize I've been up here the last three afternoons waiting for you?" she said.

He held her loosely in his arms, staring down at her. She was a very pleasant armful and all woman. "Glad to see you're still faithful," he said with a laugh.

"It's not funny!" Ella stamped her foot. "I take a chance every time I ride away from the Circle W. It's not as easy as it was to meet you here."

"You've got to admit I'm worth it, Ella."

The mocking, arrogant light she knew so well danced in Corey's eyes. He could have his way with her, and she always felt a curious weakness, a sweet lethargy creep over her when she was in his arms.

"What about me?" she said.

"You're a damned pretty girl, Ella, and you're not good for my peace of mind." He kissed her again. Her mouth was willing and her arms were willing.

"Why weren't you here yesterday?" she asked.

Corey was thankful for the shadowed dimness that filled the line cabin. He felt an uncomfortable heat in his cheeks as he repeated the same lie he had told Frazer.

Even before he had completed the explanation he

noted that she was hardly listening. She pressed against him, gripping the loose folds of his shirt in her small hands.

"Bill, let's run away," she pleaded.

"With what? We'd need a good stake."

"You could sell the ranch."

"It's mortgaged to the hilt. Besides, I owe money, and——"

She stopped him with a wave of her hand. "I know, I know. You've never had a cent and you never will."

Corey was unmoved by her passionate outburst. "You've told me that before. That's why you married Winston."

Ella's eyes screwed tight in rage. "Sometimes I hate you," she said. "If you didn't waste your time playing poker all the time and tending to your business you might have something."

"Hell, life is too short," he said.

Ella struck at him with her fists. She pounded his chest until he caught her wrists and cautioned, "Take it easy, Ella."

She strained to get free. The depth of her breathing lifted her firmly rounded breasts up and down. Her eyes were suddenly pale and hard. "Damn you, Bill," she said, "I wish I didn't love you. I—I can't stand much more. Winston's always got his hands on me." She shivered, and the flesh of her body crawled in memory of the intimacies she had had to endure.

There wasn't any break in Corey's lean cheeks. "You knew what you were doing."

"How can you be so callous about it?" Ella flared.

Corey still imprisoned her wrists. "It's too late now."

"No!" Ella's voice trembled on the thin edge of hysteria. Her eyes were very wide and very dark. "If you won't go with me, I'll go alone. I—I can't stay with Winston. Just to have him touch me, to see the way he looks at me fills me with loathing."

"All right. I'll get money," Corey said.

"When?" Ella demanded. "It's got to be soon. Tomorrow?"

Corey thought a minute. "That's kind of fast, but I reckon it can be done."

Ella frowned. Worry twisted the corners of her mouth. "Where will you get the money?"

"What do you care so long as I get it?"

"But Bill, I don't want you to——" She broke off, not sure of what shape her fears were taking.

Corey patted her shoulder. "I've got some money coming to me for a job of work." She started to ask another question, and he cut her off. "I'll get it pronto. But you've got to be sure you want to pull up stakes. Once we go there'll be no coming back."

"I know, I know, Bill." She was eager and hopeful. Anything was better than the agony of the past few days. "I was wrong, Bill. The money doesn't mean a thing if you can't stand the sight of the man you married—if you can't bear to have him touch you."

Ella's nearness set Corey's blood aboil. He realized he wanted her. The flame of desire was in him and would not be denied. And to have her he'd have to throw up everything in Two Forks. But again, with a surprising and unsparing self-analysis, he told himself he had nothing anyway. It was his chance to get out before he walked into a hang noose for rustling. Besides, Ella was worth the risk. They were two of a kind, wild and unruly and unscrupulous. They had to take what they could get out of life and to hell with tomorrow.

"Okay, Ella," he said. "How soon can you be ready to pull out?"

"Right now. I'll go the way I am."

"No. I need time to get some dinero together. Make it tomorrow. We'll meet here." Corey's boldly handsome features drew taut with concern. "But can you get away from the Circle W without being followed?"

Ella looked at Corey in a manner that was very sure and self-contained. "Leave it to me, Bill. I'll find a way." With an eager cry she flung her arms around his neck. "Bill, I'll be so glad to get away."

Once more she gave him her lips. If Corey had had any doubts about the wisdom of the course he had elected to pursue, the straining fervor of Ella's embrace was all the answer he needed. There'd be the devil to pay if there was any slip-up. The West had its own thorough way of dealing with a man who stole another man's wife. And Winston would ride from hell to breakfast to bring Ella back if he ever picked up their trail. So they'd have to move fast and far.

When Ella finally drew away Corey slid to the door. "I'll slip away first, as usual," he said. "You follow in a few minutes." Then, his face flattening out in sober gray lines, he added; "Remember. Be extra careful tomorrow leaving the ranch. I don't want anything to go wrong."

She nodded, kissed him again, and pushed him out the door. He went immediately to his horse, swung up, and rode swiftly away with a brief wave of his arm.

Ella waited a considerable interval of time before she emerged from the cabin and closed the door behind her. Excitement was a warm flood inside her. The next twenty-four hours were going to seem like an eternity. She hurried toward her horse, anxious now to get back to the Circle W before Winston or any of his hands rode in from the range.

She had mounted and was just trotting out of the trees when a horseman appeared out of the brush on the far side of the clearing. She raised her quirt, ready to slam it

100

down against the flank of her pony, when she recognized Tom Frazer.

He had saddled a horse shortly after Corey left the Double-Y spread and had then struck aimlessly toward the hills. But as he rode the thought occurred to him that he might have another look at the river ford country where the Double-Y cattle had vanished.

This time he followed a slightly different route. He had missed his way in a stretch of rough malpais and had finally wandered into a game trail that took him out on this high bench to the line cabin he hadn't visited in many months.

He was as surprised as Ella at this chance meeting. But the surprise changed to anger and suspicion when he considered what business could have prompted Ella to wander about in this rough hill country.

"So you're still seeing Bill," he said, pulling his roan to a halt beside her.

Ella smiled impudently. Her spirits were soaring wild and free now and she felt as if she could face anything—even another night with Van Winston. "How did you guess?" she queried.

"Only one reason why you'd be quartering around this section."

Ella leaned nearer. There was a provocative note in her talk and her eyes danced. "Don't tell me you're jealous, Tom."

Frazer grimaced in anger. "That's all over."

"Is it?" Ella gave him the full weight of her long-lashed eyes. They had a strong pulling power. They could be soft and infinitely deep with the warmth of a caressing hand. Or they could burn a man with withering scorn and anger. At the moment they glowed like liquid fire. "Did you forget we used to meet here?" she asked gently.

"I don't want to think about it," he said.

101

All the while they had been talking she had been studying his face. "You look like you've been having trouble," she observed. "I'll bet it was with Thorpe or some of his Big T hard cases."

"What if it was?"

"Care to talk about it?"

"No." His voice snapped at Ella like a whip. He was uncomfortable in her presence. Her animal magnetism, the womanly warmth of her made the air around Frazer hard to breathe.

Once more she flashed a sly, insinuating smile. "That means you came off second best," she said. Her eyes watched him and her talk plucked at him like a nervous, tapping finger. "The country gets tougher and tougher for the little fellow. You figure it's worth holding on?"

"Yeah, I do." Again his reply was meager and spare.

"Looks like Margo's really got you." Ella continued to smile, but some of the amusement was gone and a gray hardness clipped the corners of her moist red mouth. "Well, I wish you luck."

She lifted her reins, ready to ride off. Frazer pulled her back. "Before you go, a word of advice I've given you before," he said.

"I know," she murmured impatiently. "Leave Bill alone."

"Yeah. You're both asking for trouble. Sooner or later Winston will find out. When he does, I don't need to tell you what will happen."

Ella laughed. "Van still thinks you're the one. It's funny how he's never even suspected Bill."

Frazer hauled Ella roughly around until her face was scant inches from his own. "It's time you got some sense, Ella," he told her. "You made your choice when you married Winston. Stick to it if you don't want to get Bill killed."

"There's nothing to worry about, Tom," Ella told him, an odd, secretive light in her eyes. "Just give me a little time."

Frazer gave her a puzzled look. "What do you mean by that?"

"You'll see." She leaned out of the saddle and, without warning, kissed him on the mouth. She drew back as a horse whinnied in the brush behind them. A branch crackled. Ella glanced over Frazer's shoulder and said lightly, "Hello, Margo. Keeping tabs on your foreman?"

Margo rode into the clearing. Rage pulled the fair skin of her face in tight bands across the delicate cheekbones. She ignored Ella and spoke to Frazer. "Just another ride, Tom?"

A hot wave of blood rushed to Frazer's features. He heard Ella's faintly mocking laughter. Then she slapped her pony and galloped off into the trees.

Margo let her horse drift close to Frazer. There was a cold, stricken look in her eyes. She said in a dry, hating tone, "You don't ever give up, do you? Not even when it means breaking up a marriage."

Frazer was miserable. "It's not like you think."

"No?" Margo's manner was remote. "How is it, then?"

A taciturn grimness settled upon Frazer's bruised cheeks. He could never bring himself to implicate Corey. It was a continuing irony that Corey still remained in the clear. No one linked him with Ella. And if Margo thought he was keeping a clandestine rendezvous with Ella there wasn't anything outside of the truth that would convince her that she was mistaken. And the truth was one thing he couldn't tell her.

"I didn't meet Ella here by arrangement," he said doggedly. "You've got to believe that."

Margo's shoulders never looked wider or stiffer. She

103

was braced against him, smarting with anger and humiliation. "And if I don't?"

"Then there's nothing more to say."

Fire whipped through Frazer. There was a desolate, hungry worship in his eyes. The urge to take Margo in his arms was a hot ache sweeping along his nerves. But one look at her cold, still face told him there was no chance of that. The bars were up between them.

"I've been a fool," Margo said bitterly. "But I know when I've had enough." She swallowed as if there was a hard lump in her throat. Her tone sharpened. "From now on the Double-Y can get along without you."

A sudden spasm raced across Frazer's chest. "You mean——"

"Yes. You're fired!"

Frazer pushed the roan toward Margo. He reached for her hand. She raised her quirt threateningly and he backed away. "Get away from me." There was panic and something akin to heartbreak in the cry that was torn from her.

"Margo, you've got to listen to me," Frazer said.

"No." Her voice was adamant.

"But the ranch. You need every man now, and——"

"I'll get another man," she assured him. There was a sharp, stinging sensation at the back of Margo's eyes. She fought savagely for control. "Meanwhile, your gear will be waiting for you at the ranch."

Frazer's big jaw tightened. Temper rolled around in his vitals. "You're sure you want it this way?" he demanded.

Margo's mouth was like a bar of iron. Her answer came in a headlong rush. "Yes, this is the way I want it."

"All right." All expression went out of Frazer's face. He yanked down the brim of his sombrero. In the slanting sunlight the broad hat shadowed his bleak blue eyes. "So long," he said, and rode off—not toward town and the lower hills, but on toward the rugged ramparts of the Indian Head Mountains.

Margo was surprised at the direction he took. She raised her arm, ready to call him back. Then pride took hold of her and clamped her lips tightly together. She watched Frazer fade off into the trees and with a dry, strangled sob turned her pony about and cut back the way she had come.

10   Frazer went crashing through the trees with a reckless hard care. The irony of events that kept linking his name with Ella Winston's while leaving Bill Corey entirely free of suspicion was a maddening thing. Yet he was helpless to defend himself. And the fact that Margo had so little trust in him drove all restraint out of him.

Though he no longer represented the Double-Y ranch in any capacity, there was nothing Margo could do to stop him from continuing his own private investigations into the rustling. The theft of the Double-Y Herefords and Harry Yorke's killing had become his own personal concern. He meant to handle them in his own way. At the moment he didn't much care what happened to him in the process. He had been pushed too far. It was time to fight back.

The game he meant to play would be a perilous one. But he had lived too long with danger even to consider the risks involved. His whole body was charged with a savage, primitive excitement. He put the roan to a hard gallop.

Swinging out of the trees, he cut into a brush-filled coulee. This, in turn, would take him to a sloping stretch of malpais leading directly to the Dunbar River ford.

Once out of the defile he drew the roan to a trot, easing

the animal down the grade to the sun-dappled stream. He paused at the water's edge to study the willows on the farther bank and the rolling country that stretched beyond it.

There was no sign of any horsemen in the vicinity. The river and the ford itself had no story to tell him. Then, shifting his attention to the thick-growing brush that cluttered the near bank of the stream, Frazer decided to push into the thicket.

He couldn't have said what manner of thinking impelled him to follow the course of the river through the trees. He didn't know what he hoped to find. Certainly the cattle couldn't have been driven through the dense brush. It was slow going. Branches whipped against Frazer's face and shoulders. Thorny bushes plucked at his trousers.

After a mile of this steady slogging he was about to swing farther inland to look for easier travel when the brush thinned out. Quickly he decided to push on.

He was almost positive that the rustlers would not have driven the cattle west across the river. In that direction lay the county seat of Dunbar and a considerable number of ranches. A big risk would be run in trying to push stolen cows through carefully patrolled range. And beyond Dunbar the desert began.

No, the logical assumption must be that the rustlers had gone north with the beef. But which side of the river they had chosen for their route was a question. To the north lay the scattered battlements and numerous canyons of the Indian Heads. To the north, also, lay Guy Thorpe's holdings. If Thorpe was ramrodding the rustlers—and Frazer would have been willing to wager his life on it—then the cattle would have to be rebranded before they were pushed over the state line and sold.

Frazer recalled that his aimless search of Big T range a few days ago had been completely abortive. It had turned up nothing but legitimate Big T cows. However, there was plenty of rough country around the Big T and if he kept looking he might find something.

This trek along the river was probably foolhardy since Thorpe's men would likely swing the beef north before hitting the ford. Still, he had not found any evidence to back up this belief.

As the brush remained scattered, Frazer continued to ride close to the near bank of the river. He came, after five minutes, to a small feeder creek, splashed through the shallow water, and continued on through brush that gradually began to thicken again.

The bushes forced him to detour away from the river for several hundred yards. But in a little while he was again able to swing the roan close to the stream.

Suddenly the roan's left front hoof skidded on something slippery. The animal stumbled, throwing Frazer against the horn. The roan regained its stride and Frazer glanced idly down. What he saw made him pull the roan to a halt. He piled out of the saddle and hunkered down to examine the slender, rounded pole his mount had stumbled over. One end of the pole was jagged where it had been split off. But the other end tapered to a small handle, worn smooth by much handling.

Searching in the brush, Frazer soon came upon the other half of the broken pole. When he saw that one of the ends of this section was discolored by mud he realized that the pole had once been employed as a means of propelling a boat up or down the river. Immediately he thought of the long poles used by flatboat and barge owners in the early days of Missouri and Mississippi River travel. And with that thought came another consideration even more important.

The unusual length of the wooden shaft meant it could only have been used on some flatboat or barge. And its presence close to the river's edge signified that someone in the Two Forks country owned a flatboat. Frazer had never seen any barge traffic on the Dunbar River, since it was a shallow stream and connected with no main trade arteries. Besides, just a mile north it was broken by a falls where it narrowed precipitately to negotiate a passage through a mountain gulch.

Frazer rose from his crouched position and slowly let the broken pole slip from his fingers. Suddenly he knew how the stolen Double-Y cattle had been made to vanish. They had been loaded on flatboats from a spot near the ford and then poled upriver to some hidden landing. No doubt men were left behind to erase all tracks of the cows where they boarded the barges. Now that he considered it, he realized there was no other explanation that made sense. The scheme was virtually foolproof, and only a lucky accident had opened his eyes.

Without further delay Frazer remounted and pushed on. His job right now was to find where the cattle were unloaded. He was almost positive that the beef would only be taken far enough by boat to ditch all sign and throw off any possibility of successful pursuit.

The brush remained thick, but Frazer forced the roan through the tangle. Gradually, as he rode, a faint murmur rose on the distant air. This, he knew, was the muted roar of the falls where the land took a sudden rise as it climbed toward the higher hills.

He proceeded another quarter mile, going slowly, before he reached a narrow slough almost hidden from the river by the closely growing trees. It was barely forty feet wide and the water looked green and sluggish.

Once more he got down from the saddle. At the edge of the slough he looked into the murky depths, trying to gauge how deep the water was. The green, weed-filled surface gave no clue. Frazer broke off the branch of a sapling and thrust it into the water. He was surprised when he was unable to touch bottom with it.

All at once he was sure that this was the rustlers' unusual avenue of escape. Hurriedly he returned to the roan, caught the bridle, and led the animal along the bank of the slough. He traversed a half mile in this manner until he reached the end of the tiny inlet. And there he found what he was looking for.

A small pier had been constructed at the end of the slough. Tied up beside it and covering most of the water's surface was a big flatboat. As Frazer circled the end of the slough he came upon a smaller barge pulled half out of the water and hidden in some thick brush.

Moving cautiously forward, Frazer studied the trees on all sides of him, looking for signs of a guard. Now that he was sure he had hit upon the rustlers' secret jumping-off place he didn't want to blunder into a trap.

However, a minute's careful survey assured him that he was quite alone. He approached the pier. There he saw how scuffed and torn the gray planks were. Horses and cattle had left their marks on the splintered wood. Additional hoof sign was apparent extending up a short bare slope that led away from the slough.

Frazer climbed into the saddle again. Before going on he examined his Colt, checked the bullet load in each chamber. Then he thrust the weapon back in the leather holster which lay snugly against his right hip.

Although he saw that the trail of cattle went off at a tangent to the northeast, he now swung back toward the river. He moved on upstream until the brawling sound of the falls rose to a splashing roar. Finally he broke from a patch of trees and came out on a little shelf that showed him the lip of the cataract forty feet above him.

110

A stiff breeze whipped spray into his face as he paused to study the deep pool below the falls. The pool was ringed by ugly-looking dark rocks. Water came pouring into the circular basin in a white-laced cascade that sent spray shooting out in all directions.

Frazer backed away from the falls, curveted the roan up a slanting trail through the trees. It was a stiff climb. At one point he dismounted to lead the roan. Then, gaining higher ground, he got into the saddle once more and followed the narrow, racing course of the rapids. Here the brush thinned out again. A quarter mile farther on he almost sent the roan crashing into a rowboat half-hidden in some weeds.

The small craft, he decided, was doubtless used by the rustlers in some emergency capacity, perhaps as a means of patrolling the upper river during actual raiding operations.

Now, with a growing sense of urgency, Frazer left the river and headed inland. The thick brush gradually disappeared and he found himself in a harsh, broken land crisscrossed by canyons and ravines. He made a gradual swing back the way he had come until he picked up the trail of the cattle from the slough.

He followed it for a mile or two until the ground hardened, and again all sign vanished. On a distant high slope he saw a few grazing heads of beef but assumed they were Big T strays. Certainly Thorpe would not let any stolen critters wander around in such fashion.

Frazer realized that his task was still a monstrous one. It was logical to assume that the renegades would hide the cattle in some dead-end canyon. But which canyon? There were dozens of gulches and defiles in the area. One guess was as good as another. Yet Frazer knew he would systematically have to examine each one no matter how much time it took. There was no other way. And besides, now that he no longer was working for the Double-Y ranch, he had plenty of time.

With a bitter twist of his mouth he pushed the roan into a high-walled canyon that ran parallel to the course of the river. The hard clatter of the horse's hoofs seemed to echo thunderously from wall to wall. If there were any riders in the canyon he was certainly providing them with ample warning of his approach.

He rode for ten minutes without reaching the canyon's end and without finding any sign of grass or water, and gave it up. Doggedly he went back the way he had come and proceeded to the next canyon. This proved to be a short, dead-end affair. The third gulch he tried widened after a quarter of a mile into a small grassy basin serviced by a thin spring. Here again he met with failure.

An hour and a half went by, and the roan was beginning to tire from his long exertions, when Frazer's persistence was rewarded. He had entered a brush-choked defile about three miles from the river when he finally detected the sound of a bawling steer.

Eyes narrowing with quick interest, he pushed on through the canyon whose walls gradually fell away. Gun in hand, he rode around a slight bend and found himself in a grass-filled cup several hundred yards wide and about a half mile long. In this basin grazed a herd of cattle.

He pushed on cautiously, for the terrain was open and there was no cover to be sought if he should run into any hostile riders. A rapid survey of the grazing cattle showed him that most of the animals were Herefords. He estimated that there were about three hundred cows in the entire bunch.

The animals glanced up idly as he rode among them. Most of the Herefords carried the Double-Y brand. But about an even dozen of them had been re-branded to a Double-M. He also saw some cows that belonged to Ad

Simmons and Dale Roush. Off to one side, against a shoulder of the defile wall, were the remains of a recent branding fire.

Because he feared that the rustlers might return at any moment he decided to clear out fast. However, he still lacked one thing—proof that would definitely identify the renegades. He was sure Thorpe's Big T outfit was behind the raids. But the Double-M brand, an iron entirely new to him, did not in any way implicate Thorpe. It was probably chosen at random because it could be fashioned from a Double-Y without much effort. Other strange brands were no doubt used on the cattle belonging to Simmons and Roush. Yet none of the evidence that lay in this basin would have any actual value unless he could trap the renegades in the act of altering the brands.

There was only one thing to do: ride to town and inform the sheriff of his findings and bring the lawman back to the hills with him. After that it would be just a matter of waiting to catch the rustlers red-handed.

With that idea in mind Frazer circled wide around the grazing cows and headed for the canyon's entrance. The basin narrowed abruptly. In a matter of minutes he was riding between high rock walls along a trail barely wide enough to accommodate four horsemen riding abreast.

He was about three hundred yards from the entrance when he heard the clatter of hoofs ahead of him. Frazer's cheeks drew tight and still. He knew he was in for trouble. The defile was a trap. To go back to the basin would expose him to even greater peril, since there was absolutely no cover there. He had no way of knowing how many riders were coming toward him. But he decided he had a better chance trying to make a dash through them than turning back.

Now the hoofbeats up ahead increased their rhythm.

He knew, then, that the yonder riders had heard the roan's hoofs. Excitement pulsed heavily through him. His eyes grew bright. Then he pulled his Colt from his holster and fed steel to the roan's flanks.

The startled animal leaped forward. In a wild run the roan carried Frazer around a rocky bend in the canyon and face to face with Ray Long and the unnamed Big T puncher who had held one of his arms while Pole Richmond administered the systematic beating to him. Long was carrying a branding iron balanced across the pommel of his saddle.

Frazer jerked savagely back on the roan's reins. The animal skidded to a stop. Frazer yelled: "Grab some sky, gents!"

Ray Long muttered a curse and dropped the branding iron. But Frazer was watching the other Big T man. The latter grabbed his gun and in a rapid motion that almost defied detection sent a bullet burning past Frazer's face. That was all Frazer needed. Even as the echo of the Big T puncher's shot reverberated in the canyon Frazer laid his answering fire full upon the renegade's chest. The bullet found its mark. The puncher screamed. Then death stifled his cry and he toppled from the kack.

11 Long's face turned pasty white as he heard the thud of the heavy slug enter his companion's body. With his gun half out of the scabbard he suddenly flung his hands into the air.

"So you don't want to try your luck?" demanded Frazer. Smoke dribbled from the long barrel of his Colt. He had the hammer eared back for another shot. There wasn't any mercy in his eyes. Long saw that and refused to meet the challenge in Frazer's voice. "Throw down your gun!"

The Big T puncher carefully pulled the weapon from his holster and flung it to the ground. "All right," he said. "What's the next move?"

"Climb down and pick up that branding iron you dropped," Frazer directed. "And see that you keep away from your cutter."

The puncher dismounted. He was very deliberate in his movements and once looked back toward the canyon entrance.

"Expecting some help?" Frazer demanded as the man retrieved the branding iron and heaved his weight back in the saddle.

"Maybe," the man said. His head was cocked to one side and he seemed to be listening for something.

Pressure got into Frazer's broad shoulders. The nerve

fibers deep inside him were sending an alarm to his brain. Suddenly he knew he had to get out of the canyon.

"My friend," he said curtly, "you and I are riding into Two Forks to visit with the sheriff. I reckon you've got a little story to tell about stolen cattle."

"I won't be telling any story today," the puncher said.

"You sure of that?"

"Yeah, because you'll never get out of these hills with your hide. Here come Pole and the rest of the boys!"

An ugly light of triumph gleamed in the puncher's hooded eyes. Far off, but nevertheless distinct now, came the dim sound of approaching hoofs. Frazer's mouth settled in a thin, hard crease. Danger throbbed and grew in the ominous beat of those hoofs. Already he had lingered too long in this defile. The trap was closing, and unless he moved fast he'd be finished. He whipped his gun into line again.

"Turn your horse around and get going," he ordered the Big T puncher. "We're making a run for it."

The puncher shook his head. "I like it here."

Frazer didn't waste time. The barrel of his Colt shifted a fraction of an inch. He flipped the hammer. There was a solid crash, a pounding echo that beat solidly against them. Then the Big T puncher cried out in pain and clapped a hand to his left ear. A trickle of blood spilled through his fingers.

"Your ear is still there," said Frazer grimly, "but it won't be after my next shot. Now ride!"

The man needed no further urging. He swung his horse around and gigged him into a run. Frazer kicked the roan into motion and followed close on his captive's heels.

The clatter of their flight along the defile drowned out all other noises. Frazer couldn't tell how near those other riders were. But he made up his mind to go smashing right through them if he could.

Feverishly he inserted fresh cartridges into the fired chambers of his Colt. It proved to be an awkward task with the roan going at a dead run along the rocky trail. But he would need every bullet in the fight to come.

They burst from the canyon entrance without encountering the other horsemen. A sigh of relief escaped from Frazer. But it was short-lived. Less than a quarter of a mile away six horsemen were speeding along at a rapid clip. In the lead was Pole Richmond.

"Pole, it's Tom Frazer! Come on!" yelled the Big T puncher as he started to rein in.

Once more Frazer's gun spoke. This time he missed. But the hot slug passed so close to the puncher's face that a blind panic assailed him, and, without being ordered, he slammed his horse into a gallop.

"Try that again, friend," grated Frazer as he pounded after the puncher, "and I'll cut your backbone in two!"

A volley of gunfire erupted behind them. The slugs fell short of their target for the distance was still too great. But now, as he twisted in the saddle to look behind him, Frazer saw the Big T riders lift their horses into a straining run.

For the better part of a mile Frazer and his captive kept their lead. There was little cover in the rocky country he was traversing. Frazer hoped to reach the timber and brush that began a few miles farther south. Once in the trees he would have no trouble losing his pursuit.

But now, glancing back once more, he saw Pole Richmond wave two of his men off at a tangent. They were cutting sharply to the south, apparently anticipating his planned route of escape. And the men were gaining, too, while the roan, already ridden hard most of the afternoon, was beginning to tire.

The gap between pursuers and pursued became smaller and smaller. Six-guns began booming again. And then

117

into that general salvo of Colt fire came the flat report of a rifle. The bullet sang wickedly over Frazer's head, but it brought an added weight of worry to his strained features.

Although shooting a rifle from the back of a galloping horse was apt to be pretty much of a chance maneuver, there was always the possibility of a lucky hit bringing him down. Accordingly, Frazer bent low over the mane of the roan, urging the weary animal on in a desperate sprint. And for some minutes the roan responded and even drew away from the pursuit. The Big T man kept up without too much trouble because his horse was comparatively fresh and rested.

Just a mile to the right Frazer saw the thin line of trees and brush that marked the river above the falls. With Richmond's men bent on blocking his retreat to the south, the only way out seemed to be to angle for the river. But there was danger in that direction, too, for the brush below the falls grew in a thick tangle and would slow him up. Richmond's punchers could spread out and corner him easily.

No, the only way was to cut south and try to beat off the two Big T riders whose job it was to pin him against the river. With a savage yell, "Swing south," he slammed the roan against the Big T puncher's mount, forcing the renegade to change direction.

They rode hard with the din of six-guns and rifles becoming louder and more insistent. A brief glance to the rear showed Frazer that Richmond was the man using the rifle. Even as he looked he saw a puff of smoke issue from the long barrel and heard the angry whine of the slug speeding over his head.

Frazer was riding parallel to the river now and his line of flight carried him closer to the two riders on his flank. when there was a shout from the trees dead ahead to the He was just getting within six-gun range of the two men south. Four more men—also Big T punchers—rode into view. At a shout from the two flank riders they dug in their spurs and joined the chase.

Bitterness washed through Frazer in a dark, acid tide. He was completely cut off now. An imminent sense of the danger of his position clamped an icy hand around the nerves of his stomach. Cold perspiration greased his forehead. He was at the end of his rope. His horizons were narrowing down upon him. And in that dread moment all the hard recklessness in him, the savage will to resist, the deep core of him that had always found joy in battle, sent their stormy impulses through him. He jerked up his gun, fired at the nearest man, and saw him go down.

Then he swung the roan around, flattened out in the saddle, and went racing toward the river. The Big T puncher tried to swerve to follow him but a wild bullet drilled his mount in the chest and the man went down with the horse.

The momentary confusion gave Frazer a few precious seconds to open up a little gap between himself and the Big T reinforcements. But Richmond's main group was driving hard, the riders firing as they came, intent on killing him before he reached the river.

Frazer barely managed to stay out of pistol range. But every now and then Richmond's Winchester barked and a rifle slug went hammering by him. He could feel the roan's labored breathing. He detected a slight falter in the powerful stride. Once the animal stumbled and seemed ready to go down. But Frazer's straining voice and the touch of his boot heels in the animal's flanks sent the roan gallantly on.

The first scattered trees and brush loomed up now. Frazer plunged into their meager protection. But Richmond's bunch were right behind him, yelling wildly as they sensed Frazer's finish.

For a brief instant Frazer debated cutting sharply south into the deep tangle of underbrush that lined the lower river. But one look behind him showed him that that course was out of the question. Richmond's men were spread out in a wide skirmish line. They would trap him easily if he veered right or left. No, his only course lay straight ahead to the river.

He thought, then, of the rowboat he had seen half-concealed in the weeds and realized he was reduced to this last extremity to make his escape. It was a bleak alternative at that. The river at this point hurtled along in a narrow, rock-strewn channel that ended in the falls. Even if he gained the river without being winged by Richmond's rifle he doubted if he'd get far in the rowboat.

But, since there was no other way, he resolved to make a try at it. Urging the roan to a last, desperate sprint, he managed to pull away for a few yards. But at the river's edge the animal faltered, its front legs buckling. Before the roan went down Frazer had flung himself from the saddle and was dashing into the weeds.

He found the rowboat, but wasted frantic seconds hunting for a pair of oars. There were none to be seen. He got his hands on the craft's heavy stern and pushed the boat into the shallows. A wild yell and a withering fusillade of lead that sieved the air about him pulled him away from the boat.

The roan had staggered to its feet again. Yellow foam ringed its muzzle. Its great eyes rolled wearily in its head. The horse had been severely used and he hated to make any further demands of the animal. But he needed time. Desperately he took a few steps to the horse, slapped it smartly on the rump, and sent it plunging toward the lead group of Big T riders. The half-crazed roan crashed drunkenly into Pole Richmond's mount, almost unseating the Big T ramrod.

120

While Richmond fought to bring his piebald under control the roan caromed off into the rider beside Richmond. Into that turmoil of trumpeting horses and screaming men Frazer poured four fast shots from his Colt. Another horse went down in the melee. One man clapped a hand to his shoulder and dropped his gun.

Frazer leaped back to the rowboat. He shoved it fully into the river, waded calf-deep into the water, then scrambled aboard. Behind him the Big T riders recovered and rode furiously toward the bank. A wave of gun thunder rolled before them.

Face down across the centerboard, Frazer paddled frantically with his bare hands toward midstream. Bullets thudded into the frail craft. Two or three tore right through the weathered sides. One of them ricocheted off his boot, ripping an ugly gash in the leather. Another missed the top of his head by inches and went smashing into the wood directly below the empty oarlock.

Suddenly the fierce current of the river caught the rowboat and hurled it headlong downstream. The boat spun in a twisting arc, scraped against a rock, bounded off, and went rushing on in a whirl of white-laced spray.

Although Frazer didn't venture to lift his head above the sides he knew Richmond and the rest of the Big T punchers were spurring along the riverbank, trying to match the boat's progress. Sporadic gunfire raked the boat, then abruptly dwindled.

Frazer risked a quick glance toward shore. Thickening brush had finally impeded the forward run of the Big T riders and they'd had to pull up. But Richmond had dismounted and, with the barrel of his rifle resting across the saddle, was lining his sights on the rowboat. Frazer ducked his head again. The boat was moving faster now.

He heard the crash of the Winchester. Wood splintered beside him and a jagged sliver tore the flesh of his neck.

Then the boat reeled around a bend in the river out of range.

The roar of the approaching falls now filled the air with its dull, ominous rumbling. Frazer scrambled to a sitting position and saw at once how desperate his position was.

He was squarely in the middle of the rapids. The frail rowboat was like a live thing in the leaping waves. It rocked and heaved from side to side, twisting and turning, flung about from one capricious crosscurrent to another. Trees and brush on the shore were racing by at a rapid rate.

Frazer flung himself down again. He dipped his hands into the water, paddling in a wild frenzy to turn the boat toward shore. The effort was utterly useless. Even with a stout pair of oars he would have been unable to turn the craft. It was in the grip of a current that pushed and tugged and fumed with a dread power that would not be denied.

The boat crashed into a submerged rock with a jar that knocked Frazer down. Before he could rise his wrist was buried in water seeping through a rent in the boat's bottom. The water crept higher and higher. But the real danger lurked in the threatening lip of the falls itself just yards away.

The river now came wickedly to life. It boiled in shocking fury. A giant hand seemed to grasp the boat and hurl it forward in a screaming arc. Frazer hung on to the sides. His head whirled at the tremendous speed of the craft. A great roaring sound dinned in his ears. Through slitted eyes he saw the edge of the falls rushing forward to meet him.

In one great bound the rowboat lunged through the deep, violent trough of the rapids. It skidded over the brink into empty space, carrying Frazer with it.

12 After leaving the old line shack where he had met Ella, Corey rode back to his own spread. He was impatient to get away with Ella, yet there was little he could do until he obtained some money. And there was only one place to get that—at the Big T.

However, if he went to the Big T at this time of day he likely would find only one or two of the hands hanging around. Thorpe would be in town playing cards or out riding the hills with some of his crew.

Thinking of Richmond filled Corey with violent anger. He decided he'd have to kill Richmond. He'd felt the need for that the moment he glimpsed Frazer's bruised features. It was the one thing he could do for Frazer to atone for a long cycle of treachery and deception, the memory of which now sickened him.

Back at his own ranch Corey cleaned out the drawers of his desk, destroying all worthless papers. The place was run-down. He would be leaving nothing valuable behind him. He fed his saddle stock, checked the running gear on the buckboard he meant to use for the dash to the railroad the following night. There was a nine-o'clock train passing westward through Dunbar. If he and Ella caught it they'd be well out of the state by dawn and too far for any pursuit to nail them.

Finally, late in the afternoon, Corey threw his rig on a

powerful dun gelding and rode toward the hills. He avoided all the main roads and trails, not wishing to meet anyone on this journey.

The purple shadows of dusk were crawling down the hills when he rode into the Big T ranch yard. Only a few horses scampered around in the corral. By that he knew that most of the Big T crew were still abroad. Guy Thorpe stamped out onto the veranda when Corey racked up his pony at the hitching rail alongside the house.

"What brings you here, Corey?" Thorpe queried, a slight edge in his voice.

Corey didn't answer until he had mounted the steps and stood beside the heavily built rancher. Then he said, "Let's talk inside."

Thorpe gave him a queer, intent glance, then shrugged and walked into the spacious but barely furnished front room. A lamp with a smoke-grimed chimney stood on a table near an old roll-top desk. A worn rug covered the crudely boarded floor. There was a torn leather sofa, a few straight-backed chairs, an Indian blanket tacked to the far wall. And beside the desk was a crude iron safe.

"Let's have it," said Thorpe, pausing near the table to riffle the pages of a musty mail-order catalogue.

"I want two things," said Corey, his voice dead level. "The first is Pole Richmond."

Thorpe closed the catalogue, his eyes suddenly alert and wary. "What do you want him for?"

Hot blood pumped through the thick, swelling cords of Corey's neck. He said flatly, "I'm going to kill him."

Thorpe tensed. His right hand was poised like a predatory claw over his holstered six-shooter. Then the steel-bright glitter in Corey's eyes plucked at his attention and he laughed raucously. "I reckon you've seen your good friend, Tom Frazer."

"I have," snapped Corey. "That's why Richmond is go-

124

ing to die." He stopped, and the fury in him sharpened his tone. "Tom's face looked as if a team of horses had walked over it. If I'd known he'd taken that kind of beating I'd have called Richmond on it last week while we were on that cattle drive."

Thorpe drew himself up to his full height. As all daylight faded in the yard the illumination from the guttering lamp turned stronger. It outlined the heavy shadows along Thorpe's cheekbones. "You figure you're big enough to handle Richmond?" he inquired.

"Yeah," grated Corey furiously, "and anybody else that lays a hand on Frazer."

"Of course, stealing cattle from the ranch he ramrods is all right in your book," taunted Thorpe.

"Forget that," Corey said. "I'm kind of late, but not too late to straighten a few things out. Which reminds me that you owe me five hundred dollars for my share in that stolen-cattle sale Richmond made the other day."

Thorpe's knife-thin lips twisted in a faint smile. "You'll have to wait awhile."

"I want it now."

"The money isn't here."

Corey's skin drew taut over his jawbone. "What about the safe?"

"It's empty," said Thorpe. His broad shoulders were a little round at the edges now. Wariness flickered increasingly in his eyes.

"Suppose we have a look, Guy," Corey said, his tone gentle as a summer wind, yet overlaid with a definite threat. "While we're at it you can pay me my share in that raid on the Double-Y the other night."

All the overbearing insolence that was in Thorpe's nature now cropped up in his talk. "You've got your gall, Corey. I'll pay you when I'm damned good and ready."

Corey leaned forward. He fixed his narrowed eyes like

125

a hot steel drill on the rancher. "Maybe you didn't hear me, Guy," he said. "I want to be paid tonight—right now."

The ugly promise of violence stirred the close air of the room. Thorpe's mouth twitched. A mean look stole over his cheeks. "You don't give me orders. I still run the Big T."

"Run it and be damned!" Corey literally flung the words into the rancher's face. "But you still owe me money. I figure it to be a thousand altogether."

"Why the hurry? Another poker game?" Thorpe's question was tinged with mockery and definitely unfriendly.

"No, I'm pulling out," said Corey.

Thorpe showed unbelieving surprise. "Say that again."

"You heard me."

Thorpe's nostrils quivered. His eyes were suddenly red and wicked. "Nobody pulls out of this game unless I say so."

They were getting nearer and nearer the breaking point. Each man knew it. Every nerve in Corey's body screamed a warning. Thorpe's big body bowed a trifle more. His elbow was hooked. He was ready to dive for his gun at Corey's first move.

Corey remained immobile. The seconds dragged on with almost interminable slowness. He wasn't afraid of Thorpe. He had no liking for the man and was coldly agreeable to trading lead with him. But he was enough of a realist to understand that if he matched shots with Thorpe now he might forfeit his chance to kill Richmond. And, for the moment, Richmond was more important.

However, Corey did not hesitate with his reply to the Big T owner. "You may run this outfit but you don't run me. I'm a free agent."

"That's where you're wrong," Thorpe told him. He was

completely cold and antagonistic. "Nobody quits in this game. That includes you. You know too much. The only way you or anybody else will pull out is feet first. Is that understood?"

There is a point beyond which no man can be pushed. Suddenly Corey knew he had reached his limit. He had gone too far with Thorpe to back down. It was fight or crawl—and he'd rather die than crawl. Also, he knew, with a shocking sense of clarity, that his entire plan of escape hinged on what he did in the next few seconds.

Thorpe had no intention of paying him his share of the rustling loot until he felt like it. But he had to have it tonight. And Corey knew that if he wanted Ella and wanted his money he'd have to forget Richmond and have his go at Thorpe.

"Do you figure you can make that stick?" Corey asked while excitement poured through him in a torrid tide of sensation. He felt all his muscles tighten up. His chest seemed to be on fire. But he was ready—ready to go all the way.

Guy Thorpe's sneering smile hit Corey like a slap in the face. "Why don't you try me and see?" he murmured.

The ball of fire in Corey's chest burst. His right hand streaked toward his gun, then stopped as his fingers closed around the stock. A party of horsemen drummed into the yard. They made a fierce clatter. Corey jumped to one side, fearing that Thorpe would complete his draw. But the rancher let his Colt slide back into the leather rest.

"Change your mind?" Thorpe asked.

Corey backed against the wall, hearing the thump of boots on the veranda steps. He had declared his intentions to Thorpe, and it occurred to him, with a dismal sense of regret, that he'd made a mistake in not forcing the issue before the arrival of the Big T crew. Thorpe would never let him out of the place alive.

But if he understood that he gave no sign of it when he said to Thorpe, "I was forgetting about Richmond."

He turned his attention to the doorway. He laughed derisively when the Big T owner called loudly, "We've got company, Pole."

The tall, lanky ramrod strode into the room with his hand on his gun. He saw Corey at once, glanced swiftly over to Thorpe, noticing that the latter's fingers still rested near the stock of his Colt. Behind Richmond came Ray Long and two other men. The rest of the crew could be heard talking and shouting as they dismounted at the corral.

"What's going on here, Guy?" Richmond asked. "You look like you're ready to eat Corey."

Thorpe gestured Richmond across the room to a spot where he would be flanking Corey. Long and the other two men spread out in like manner, eyes intent on Corey. They all sensed that something was wrong.

"Corey can wait," said Thorpe, looking not at Richmond but at Corey, "until I find out what kept you so long."

"We ran into some trouble in the hills—with Frazer," said Richmond. "He stumbled on our cattle hideout."

"You're sure of that?" Thorpe demanded.

"Hell, we saw him riding out of the canyon where the critters have been grazing."

Thorpe's eyes darkened. "I reckon you'd better let me have the whole story right from the beginning."

"Not much to it," said Richmond. "We were going up there to rebrand some of that stolen Double-Y beef. Long and Harkins rode ahead. They ran into Frazer in the canyon as Frazer was coming out. Harkins made a play for his gun and Frazer drilled him."

128

"What about you, Ray?" asked Thorpe. "What were you doing while all the shooting was going on?"

Long's triangular features filled with a rush of blood. "I was toting a running iron," he said. "By the time I got rid of it and went for my cutter Frazer had the drop on me."

Thorpe snorted in disbelief. "Why don't you say you didn't have sand enough to draw against him?" Then he ignored the puncher and swung back to Richmond. "All right. Get on with it."

"Well," said the ramrod, "according to Ray, Frazer intended to take him into town and make him talk about that stolen beef to the sheriff."

"That would have fixed us fine," snapped the rancher. "But you took care of Frazer?"

"Just about."

Thorpe's eyebrows drew together. "What does that mean?"

"We chased him to the river." Richmond's voice was curt and sharp, as if he resented having to explain his actions. "He tried to run through us and ride south but we pinned him to the river. He got into that old rowboat we've been keeping in the bushes and was carried down to the falls."

"Didn't you follow him?" Thorpe demanded.

"No need to do that. The falls finished him."

"How do you know? Did you see him smashed on the rocks?"

Richmond's voice rose in anger. "Hell, nobody could swim away after hitting those rocks below the falls. You know that. We tried to bring him down with gunfire. But he was lucky."

Thorpe looked worried and displeased. "Maybe his luck held going over the falls, or maybe he managed to row to shore."

"He went over, I tell you," snapped the ramrod.

129

"There were no oars in the boat. We saw the current catch the boat and carry him down the rapids. He's done."

"I don't like it," said Thorpe. "We'd better move the cattle in the morning. And those barges in the slough——"

"Stop worrying, Guy," Richmond told him. "Where Frazer is now he'll do no more talking."

Corey, a silent witness to all this talk, suddenly broke his silence. Thorpe and the others had temporarily forgotten him. Now Corey made a lightning-fast move and dragged out his two Colts.

"I figure you'll be keeping Tom company in a few minutes," he said with a dull savagery. His hands tightened around the stocks of his forty-fives. "Don't anybody move or Richmond dies right now."

Thorpe slid away one step from his desk, then stopped at a warning glitter in Corey's eyes. Richmond's right elbow crooked, the fingers of his arm fanned out widely. But he didn't attempt to draw. His gaunt, sallow cheeks took on a gray tinge.

"What's in your craw, Corey?" he asked tightly.

Thorpe laughed. "Can't you guess, Pole? He's squaring accounts for Frazer."

"That's right, Richmond," said Corey. "You've got it coming. Tom was the best friend a man ever had. I've treated him like dirt. But by God you're going to pay for that beating you gave him and for sending him to his death."

Corey paused, his features like sun-bleached parchment. Rage and grief gnawed at his vitals like a corroding poison. Tom Frazer had always seemed too much of a man to die. He was like a rock—something that was always there, solid and invincible. But now he was dead, and the man who had sent him to his doom was just a few feet away from Corey. That fact was like the point of a knift twisting and tearing at his flesh and nerves.

"Richmond," he said in a voice turned utterly strange by fury, "I'm going to give you a chance to draw, though by rights I ought to shoot you down as you stand."

The ramrod's mouth twisted in a leer. "Corey, I'll be damned glad to accommodate you."

"Forget it," said Thorpe. "There are five of us. They're comfortable odds. You don't know it, Pole, but Corey wants to quit us. He came here for a pay-off. I reckon we can give it to him—in lead."

Corey grinned. It was an ugly grin, without humor. Sheer destructiveness was in him. He was primed to kill. His gray, mask-like face, his thinly creased lips, the utterly cold eyes told the Big T riders that.

"You can name the play, Guy," Corey said. "But just remember I've got my sights lined on Richmond. If you or anybody else goes for a gun Richmond dies. After that I don't give a damn!"

Black malevolence ripped through Thorpe. He set himself for action. His shoulders bent, his head tipped forward. Richmond's cry arrested him. "Hold it, Guy!" A tremor shook his long, gangling body. He said to Corey: "What's the alternative?"

"Everybody but you throws his guns to the floor," said Corey. "Then I'll holster mine and we'll both start from scratch."

"Do you take us for fools?" growled Thorpe. "Once we're disarmed you could shoot us all full of holes. Nothing doing. We'll——"

"Wait, Guy!" Richmond interrupted, fear swimming muddily in his eyes. "I want a chance to fight back. I won't get it unless you and the others toss in your cutters."

For a second or two no one spoke. The silence was like

131

a power drill, slashing at their nerves. Dark forces, turgid and ugly, whirled unseen in the hot, close room. Every man stood rooted, looking for some signal from Thorpe. The walls seemed to swell outward, waiting for the crash of guns, the thump of bullets.

Thorpe froze. He was dry-lipped and tightly coiled like a steel spring. A wild appetite blazed in his hooded dark eyes. When he spoke it was in an enraged whisper. "You win, Pole. He's all yours." His hand moved toward his Colt.

"Wait!" ordered Corey. "I'll say when." His eyes slid toward Long. "You first, Ray. Lift your gun clear and toss it on the floor."

Long followed instructions to the letter. In similar fashion the other two Big T punchers were forced to disarm themselves. Then Corey said to Thorpe, "You're next, Guy."

The rancher took his gun out of the holster. His movements were slow, and he watched the barrel of Corey's left-hand Colt. Thorpe leaned forward to chuck his weapon away from him and, without warning, hurled himself to one side. Even as he crashed to the floor his gun was spewing flame.

Corey fired at almost the same instant. But he was a split second late. His bullet sped through the area where Thorpe had been standing and cascaded into the far wall. With his right-hand gun he lined a shot at Pole Richmond just as Thorpe's bullet ripped into the flesh of his side.

The jarring blow knocked Corey off his feet. It distorted his aim enough so that he missed Richmond. The lanky ramrod lunged behind the table, his long-barreled Colt leaping into his fist and spilling a hot cylinder of lead inches past Corey's ear.

In that dread moment Corey had a swift vision of his own destruction. Everything had gone wrong. Thorpe and

Richmond had him caught in a wicked crossfire, and in another second the remaining two Big T punchers would join the fracas.

Half-sprawled on the puncheons, Corey tilted his right-hand gun around and smashed the coal-oil lamp with a single shot. Darkness dropped like a heavy curtain upon the smoke-filled room. He rolled frantically to his left as Thorpe fired at the muzzle flare from Corey's gun.

The room shook to the roar of Colts. Corey dismally watched the bright red flame streaks issue from four separate places in the darkness and knew the other two Big T punchers had retrieved their weapons.

He had to get out before he was cut to ribbons by slashing lead. But his first effort to rise dragged a low groan from him. His entire right side seemed to be on fire. There was a sticky warmth in the region of his belt buckle and he realized it was blood. Pain was like a hammer driving steel splinters into his lacerated flesh.

He had only two avenues of escape. The front door, which now showed as a gray stain against the room's deep background of blackness, and the side window which was commanded by Thorpe. The agony beating through him and the sickness it brought with it warned Corey that the nearest way was the only way. That meant he'd have to go through the doorway. But the moment he moved into the shaft of dim gray light from outside he'd be a clear target for Big T bullets.

Weariness crept slowly and inexorably along his muscles. He felt wrung out and useless. But somehow he had to muster the energy to make a dash for the door. Thorpe and the others kept up a sporadic fire, shifting craftily after each shot so they would not be caught by a return from Corey.

"Pole," Thorpe yelled suddenly. "Watch the door!"

Richmond was too wise to answer and give away his

133

position. Corey was tempted to drill a shot toward Thorpe's corner of the room, then changed his mind. Instead, he cocked his left-hand gun, gripped his right-hand weapon tightly in his fist, and set himself to rise.

Crouched on one knee with the warm flow of blood seeping down his right hip, Corey flung his left-hand gun toward the window. At the exact moment of impact with the floor the bullet under the hammer exploded in a crashing roar.

Immediately the Big T men concentrated their fire on the spot.

"Burn him down!" Thorpe shouted.

Corey pushed himself to his feet. A fierce jab of pain rocketed through him. Nausea welled in his stomach. He felt lightheaded. But he literally threw himself through the open doorway. He was halfway across the veranda when Thorpe's strident yell rose in the room.

"He's gone through the door!"

The yell was followed by a volley of six-gun slugs that tore through the open doorway. But Corey was already down, having stumbled at the head of the stairs. He went bouncing down the wooden steps, each jolt racking him with excruciating pain. And as he hit the dust of the yard on his back he heard the tramp of boots pounding toward him from the room. At the same instant a shout from the bunkhouse announced the approach of the rest of Thorpe's gun-slick crew.

134

13 Frazer let go of the sides of the rowboat the instant the river spun the tiny craft over the lip of the falls. He felt the boat plunge away from him. Then he, too, was plummeting downward. A cold, mist-laden wind pelted his face. It sucked the air out of his lungs. He blacked out for a second. But consciousness came roaring back when his hurtling body smashed through the boiling torrent of water at the base of the cataract.

He went down into cool green darkness shot through with a riot of bubbles. His shoulder jarred against a hidden rock. The entire left side of his body went numb. He cracked an elbow against another boulder. Then he was fighting to rise to the surface against the pounding pressure of a wall of water cascading down from the lip of the falls.

He got clear, gasping for breath. But at once a vicious current sucked him into the edge of a vortex. He was spun around at a dizzy rate. The world became a gyrating bowl. The walls of the bowl were a mountain of slashing white-combed water. Above it was the drumming curtain of the falls itself, heaping its tons of water into the pool in the steady, inexorable manner of ocean waves pounding a sandy beach.

Frazer was whirled around the outer edges of the bowl. A half-dozen times he made the dizzy circuit before he was sent lurching down into the funnel. He gave himself up then. A green tide overwhelmed him. Water was all around him. It was a ceaseless pressure. It squeezed his lungs like a bellows. Then a capricious current caught him and flung him clear.

He broke through the surface of the pool with his lungs on fire with pain. A desperate, flailing hand struck a huge board floating past his face. It proved to be a piece from the side of the rowboat. A look around showed him a few other sections of the craft. It had been shattered on the rocks close against the wall of the falls. That he had escaped a similar fate could only be attributed to the fact that he had been flung outward away from the falls itself when the boat went over the brink.

Frazer tried to hang onto the board in an effort to regain his strength. But the piece of wood was too light to sustain his weight. Feeling himself about to submerge once more, he struck out desperately for the black rocks that formed a ragged, protecting wall around the pool. With the left side of his body still numb from his collision with the sunken boulder he was barely able to make forward progress.

He was exhausted by the time his knee scraped against some stones and he staggered through the shallows. The stones were slippery and he lost his footing and went down among the larger rocks that lined the bank. He banged his side, jolted his shoulder again. But he was too weary to care. He slumped down in the ankle-deep water and lay there.

All the energy that was in him had been used up. He was as limp as a rag. He felt as if he'd never be able to take another step. His body was a mass of aches. Other rocks at the bottom of the pool had punished his flesh but he hadn't noticed them because of the shocking blow he'd taken in the shoulder.

Ten minutes went by before he was able to muster the strength to get up and clamber stiffly over the remaining rocks to the grassy bank beyond. Once more he sank down to rest. His wet clothes felt clammy on his body. His red hair hung in an unruly cowl over his still-swollen face. Wearily he dragged off his boots, emptied the water out of them, and struggled into them again.

He got up slowly, looking carefully across the pool to the yonder brush. If the Big T riders had followed him along the rapids they might even now be quartering through the trees toward him. The danger forced him to retreat into the trees at his back. There he paused long enough to empty his gun and clean the bullet loads with leaves before replacing them in the Colt cylinder. It was a makeshift arrangement and he doubted if the weapon would be useful in an emergency.

A look at the sun told him that darkness was not far off. He was about twenty miles from the Double-Y ranch and on foot he'd be lucky if he reached the outfit by the next afternoon. He was in rough, hilly country and the high-heeled boots he wore were not meant for walking.

He realized that by this time Richmond's riders would have appropriated his gelding. The only place he could secure another mount was at the Double-Y ranch. The thought galled him because he'd counted on reaching the sheriff by nightfall to initiate action against Thorpe's Big T outfit. Now, even though Richmond's bunch most likely would think him dead, Thorpe might spook up enough to change the hiding place of the stolen cattle. However, there were still the barges—though they would not definitely link Thorpe to the rustling. The only sure way was to lead a posse up into these hills and catch Thorpe's men with the stolen beef.

Impatience drove Frazer to a fast gait through the timber. Yet he held the pace for only a short time. The going was too rough. There were too many steep pitches to climb and the ache in his shoulder had by no means subsided enough to allow him complete freedom of movement.

When night fell he made a dry camp under a low overhang at the base of a bluff almost completely shrouded by bushes. Because the chill in the air was more pronounced he decided to risk a fire in order to dry his clothes. The matches he carried were useless so he had to resort to the age-old wilderness method of igniting a tiny blaze among some dry scraps and twigs by rubbing two sticks together. Once he had the fire going well he shed his clothes and hung them up to dry on the branch of a nearby sapling. When they were dry he put them on again, added some wood to the fire, stretched out on the ground close to the flames, and drifted off to sleep.

He spent a thoroughly uncomfortable night. Though his body ached with weariness the chill forest air and his lack of a blanket rendered it impossible for him to sleep soundly. The ground was cold on his back and he was forced to rise at intervals to replenish the fire.

When morning came he felt worse than he did the night before. There was a cramped stiffness in all his limbs. Hunger, too, had added its own pressing demands upon his tired system. He hadn't touched food since the previous noon and the physical energy he had expended had drained him dry. He was a big man and an active one. His powerful body required generous quantities of food to keep it going. But he had to face the grim fact that he wouldn't be eating again until sometime in the afternoon when he reached the Double-Y spread.

It wasn't a happy prospect. He stamped out the embers of his campfire, scattered the ashes in the dirt, and moved off through the trees on a journey that threatened to tax all his remaining endurance.

138

He walked all of that morning, stopping at half-hour intervals to rest his feet which had begun to issue an aching protest after the first few miles. The country lost some of its rougher contours as he dropped down into the lower foothills. But to Frazer, stumbling along in his high-heeled boots, there was no alleviating the pain that each step brought, no halting the exhaustion which steadily overcame him.

He began to lose all trace of time. The brassy sun passed its zenith and started its downward wheel through the blue, cloud-packed sky. Dust lifted in a gray, smothering swarm around him as he traversed a dry arroyo. It settled on the streaks of sweat that slid down his cheeks and formed a soft crust on his skin.

There seemed to be no end to the undulating sweep of hills and ridges. The muscles of his thighs gathered in great knots, throbbing and twisting at each long stride. His feet were on fire inside his boots. The flesh of his toes was rubbed raw by friction. He wanted to stop and take off his boots. But if he did, he'd never get them on again.

It was close to five o'clock in the afternoon when he first sighted the Double-Y ranch. For the past two hours his progress had been agonizingly slow. Three times he had fallen. Each time the effort to rise had taken a greater surge of his will. The powerful body that had carried him through more than one rough-and-tumble fight was being relentlessly hammered down. Only a thin spark kept it going.

Frazer was a mile from the ranch when he first saw the main house. He tried to speed up his pace but stumbled and fell to his knees. He rose slowly. Every nerve, every muscle in his whipcord frame felt bruised and beaten. It was as if some unseen force beyond him had stretched them taut and was cruelly plucking at them with a steel hook.

He shuffled down the slope of the last ridge. The trail he left was a ragged one. Through weary, bloodshot eyes he surveyed the yard. It looked empty. Cooper and White were probably still out on the range somewhere. But Margo ... Like the twist of a knife the thought of her shot a wild impulse through him. This was a grim return. He didn't expect any welcome. He didn't relish asking any favors. Yet he had no choice in the matter.

The sight of the well fifty yards from the house pulled Frazer that way. He hadn't had a drink since he splashed through a narrow brook shortly after noon. Now he stumbled over to the well and tugged at the chain attached to the bucket resting in the cool, shaded depths. The chain creaked as he laboriously hauled the bucket up and rested it on the well fender. He took down the big tin cup hanging from a nail and dipped it into the bucket.

He had gulped down his second cupful of water when he became aware of someone watching him. He dropped the cup into the bucket and turned to face the ranch house. Margo was there. Just that glimpse of her leaning against the railing, her fair head tipped toward him, filled him with a pang of loneliness and want.

Frazer searched for some sign of a break in the rigid composure of Margo's face. There was none. The pressing weight of her unfriendly gaze gave him no quarter.

"If you've come for your bedroll," she said severely, "you'll find it on your bunk."

"All I want is a horse right now," he murmured.

He walked out of the shade into the sun, blinking his eyes in the fast-fading light. His step was rocky and uneven.

Margo stiffened suddenly. Her glance became intent. She looked across the yard and over toward the corral. "Where's your gelding?"

"Up in the hills." His mouth twisted bitterly. "Sorry

about that. You can have mine in exchange—the roan, I mean. But now I'd like to take that roan for a little while."

The emptiness in Frazer's belly was like a live crawling thing. He seemed to be one mass of knotted tissue. He had never been so hungry but he knew now he wouldn't tell Margo that. He wanted to fall down right where he stood, but pride carried him across the yard toward the corral.

Suddenly Margo cried out to him. He didn't turn around. He kept walking. The corral still seemed very far away. But he had to reach it. He had to get a rope around his favorite roan.

Then Margo came up behind him. She caught him by the arm, pulled him around. The abrupt motion propelled Frazer off balance. He fell against her. Margo gasped, seeing for the first time the haggard, washed-out look in Frazer's dust-streaked face.

"Tom!" she said, holding him near with the strength of her arms. "You're hurt!" Her face went white.

"Not hurt," he said. "Just tired from walking."

"Where did you lose your horse?"

"A mile above the falls."

Shock put a pale glow in Margo's eyes. "Tom—you didn't walk all the way from the falls?"

He nodded curtly and tried to pull away.

"Tom, wait!" Margo said. "Oh, my dear! You look as if you're ready to drop. What happened? Tell me!"

Weary as he was, he wanted to crush Margo in his arms. He wanted her lips hard against his. But all he said was, "You're forgetting I don't work for the Double-Y any more."

Margo looked fully at him. She hadn't wanted to admit how deeply affected she was by his sudden appearance. The day for her had been horribly bleak and lonely. More than once she told herself she was a fool for sending him away. Whether he still loved Ella or not, she should have taken whatever he offered. A little of him was better than nothing at all.

Now she saw once and for all what she had long been too blind to see. Frazer was the one thing that mattered to her. He could have her if he wanted her. All of her, or any part of her. Just having him back on any terms was better than the emptiness she had been saddled with after he had ridden off the afternoon before.

"Tom," she said with sudden tenderness, "I'm sorry. I'm glad you're back. I—I don't care about Ella or anything else. I—I want you here." Her arms slipped around him and she kissed him, not minding the dust on his face, the stubble of his beard that bit like tiny needles into the soft skin around her mouth.

She pulled away abruptly, conscious of the fatigue that was in him. "Tom, you're worn out. You've got to sit down. When did you eat last?"

Bewildered by the change in her, Frazer said slowly, "At noon yesterday."

Margo started in surprise. "That's more than twenty-four hours. And you've walked more than twenty miles." She caught him by the arm, pulled him toward the house. "You must sit down and rest. I'll make something to eat."

He walked dazedly beside her. But despite the hunger and the weariness that assailed him he was still nagged by the necessity of getting on to town. "Hurry, Margo. I've got to go on to Two Forks."

She stopped at the front door of the ranch house. "What were you doing at the falls and how did you lose your horse? I want to know."

Frazer replied bluntly, "I found your stolen Herefords."

"Tom, you didn't!" Margo was incredulous.

He nodded wearily. "In a blind canyon above the falls. And I found some of Thorpe's bunch on the way to re-brand some of the beef."

A pleased excitement heightened the color in Margo's cheeks. "I'm so glad," she murmured. Then her face sobered when she saw how he leaned against the wall, how his body sagged, limp with fatigue. "Here, sit down," she said, and pushed open the door and directed him to a chair.

Frazer slumped into the chair. A ragged sigh escaped him. Now, sitting down, waves of exhaustion broke over him in a warm, cloying tide.

"I'll hurry and get together something to eat," Margo told him. "Then I want to hear what happened and what you intend to do."

She left him and went off to the kitchen. When she returned in ten minutes she found him asleep in the chair, his chin sunken on his chest, his long body sprawled out.

Deep lines of remorse appeared about the girl's nose and mouth when she stared down at Frazer's dusty, bedraggled figure. She wondered, with a stab of guilt, what he had gone through up in the hills. Once again he had played the role of a lone wolf. Once again, she guessed, he had come close to death. And always the risks he ran were for her and the Double-Y ranch.

She went back to the kitchen, pushed the frying pan filled with steak and potatoes to the back of the stove. She let Frazer sleep until Tex White rode in from the range and entered through the rear door to inquire if Margo had any special orders for him.

The heavy thump of White's boots on the floor and his strident yell, "What are you doing here, Tom?" pulled Frazer out of the deep well of slumber.

He stirred dazedly. His arms waved in front of his face as if he were groping through fog. "Hello, Tex," he murmured thickly, and got stiffly to his feet. A glance through the window showed him it was almost dark. "Why did you let me sleep?" he asked Margo.

"Tom, you need the rest."

"I've got to be going," he said doggedly.

Margo came forward and took him by the arm. "Not before you sit down and eat and tell me about the Double-Y cattle."

"What's up?" demanded White eagerly. "Did you get a line on that rustled beef, Tom?"

Frazer allowed himself to be led into the kitchen. He sank down wearily on a chair. Margo hurried to the stove. She took the frying pan, emptied the contents onto his plate. Then she filled a big cup with steaming black coffee.

Frazer picked up a fork and started eating. For ten minutes he didn't speak. The food disappeared rapidly from his plate. He drained the coffee cup. Margo refilled it. Only then did Frazer pause to recount his adventures up around the falls.

"Tom, you take such desperate chances," Margo said when he had finished. "And you went alone."

"Better that way," he said. "Less chance of being spotted."

"But think what happened," Margo insisted. "Why, it's a miracle you survived that spill into the falls pool."

"By God, that must have been something!" murmured White, a glint of admiration in his eyes.

"I'm not likely to forget it," said Frazer, and bent to his food again.

When he had emptied the second cup of coffee he pushed back his chair and stood up. He moved away from the table, but grimaced as he took a step.

"Your feet are giving you hell, I reckon," White observed.

Frazer paused, rocking back on his heels. "I'll have to change clothes, then ride out."

"But what can you do tonight?" Margo asked.

"I want to get a sheriff's posse organized to ride into the hills," Frazer told her. "Richmond and Thorpe probably figure I'm dead. But if I know Thorpe, he'll play it safe and move that beef to some other hiding place. I aim to prevent that. If I can get a bunch to hit for the hills tonight we can be in position tomorrow to trap the Big T crowd when they try to shift that beef. That'll be enough for Sheriff Landon to act on."

Frazer moved toward the door.

"Anything I can do?" White asked.

Frazer turned around. "Yeah. You can take a *pasear* east of town and try to round up some of the boys from Simmons's and Roush's ranch. When you get them ride on to town and meet me there. I'll rout out Lovelock and Bassett and go on to Two Forks for Landon. You ought to be able to make town with the Simmons and Roush crowd in a little more than two hours. Meet me there."

14   Corey scrambled frantically to his feet at the foot of the veranda steps. The Big T crew were rushing toward the house, their shouts kicking up a great racket in the yard. He was in a tight spot. The next few seconds would tell his story.

With a savage curse framing his lips Corey lifted his gun and fired two fast shots into the open doorway of the ranch house. A scream of pain floated back to him. There was a wild scramble as Richmond, Thorpe, and the others fell back.

Corey twisted around and stumbled toward the end of the veranda, meaning to put the rest of the Big T crew on the far side of the ranch house from him. Pain slogged through him at every step. Twice his leg buckled and he was almost thrown to the ground.

He was breathing hard and fast when he reached his pony. He got one foot into the stirrup, tried to heave his body into the saddle. A sharp burst of agony in his wounded side drove him gasping to his knees. A Big T man appeared on the veranda, pumping a shot toward him. Corey, half-rising, fired back. The Big T puncher dropped behind the railing.

Again Corey put a foot in the stirrup. He could hear the yells of the rest of the crew as they charged around the front of the house. They would be upon him in another moment. Desperation drove Corey to a supreme effort. He almost went blind with pain but he hauled himself into the saddle, kicked the pony into motion.

Bullets spattered the leaves of the tree over his head as he sped away. The Big T crew had rounded the veranda and every man was pumping hot lead in his direction. Richmond and Thorpe and the others joined in, their long-barreled Colts adding their noise to the unholy din.

"Don't let him get away!" Thorpe yelled.

But Corey was already out of six-gun range. The cottonwoods that gave shade to the yard during the hot hours of the day thinned out. Corey spurred his pony across the open plain.

Behind him Pole Richmond shouted to the Big T crew. "Get your horses!"

Feverishly Corey reloaded his Colt. His hands were unsteady from the pounding gait of his horse and from the insidious weakness that was creeping like paralysis over his muscles. At last the job was done, and he thrust the weapon into his holster. After that he gave his entire attention to his riding. And the farther he went the greater an effort it became.

Dizziness sloshed around in his head. The torn flesh in his side felt as if a red-hot branding iron was riveted there. He found it difficult to breathe. His eyes seemed to be out of focus. The distant trees for which he was aiming did a crazy war dance in front of him.

A muted thunder well to the rear warned him that the Big T pursuit was under way. Still the timber belt seemed terribly far away. He grew fainter and hotter. Once he swayed and almost toppled out of the saddle. Only a last-minute grab for the horn saved him. The pain in his side had become a heavy, monotonous pulse. It was a drumbeat in his head, dulling his senses.

He looked back. Far to the rear a bunch of riders was

147

strung out. He could see them like a waving black rope under the night's gray starshine. When he swung around again blackness swam into his brain. He slumped forward. Instinctively his arms encircled his pony's neck. The coarse mane enveloped his face.

The pony trotted on, Corey's head bouncing up and down at each long stride. The trees drew near, but now the pony's gait had slackened. Just a scant mile to the rear Pole Richmond and his gun slicks hammered along at a powerful run. Yard by yard they gained on Corey.

Two hundred yards from the timber line Corey fought his way out of the cloying fog of unconsciousness. At once he was made aware of the throbbing hole below his ribs. He could feel the warm wash of blood and knew that each lurch of his body in the saddle sent another fraction of his life spurting out of the wound. That would go on inexorably until there was no blood and no life in him.

If he could reach the trees he might have a chance. He realized he couldn't stick in the saddle much longer. His legs were getting weak. He was losing his grip on the pony's barrel. The dizziness was coming back. He shook his head doggedly, trying to fight it off. A trip hammer was at work above his eyes. It sent nails of pain through his head. With each heavy blow the nails drilled deeper.

Suddenly the timber was at hand. The pony plunged into a narrow, twisting trail. Corey roused himself enough to slam his heels into the animal's flanks. The pony responded with a burst of speed. But the added jolt increased the tempo of the trip hammer that now seemed to be punishing every section of his body.

The trail lifted in a long slope. The pony took the grade in full stride. Somewhere behind him, still on the prairie, Corey heard the racket of pursuit. The Big T would not give up. They wanted his scalp. And they meant to have it. There was an ugly blood lust in the grim, pursuing cry they sent pealing through the night.

A small break appeared in the thick brush. On an impulse Corey swung his gelding off the trail. He pushed the animal into the opening. It was only a few yards deep. But he forced the panting, struggling horse into the tangle of the trees and brush. Low branches whipped against him. He had all he could do to hold on. Deeper and deeper the horse plunged. Then Corey pulled the gelding to a halt.

He would have dismounted but was afraid to risk the noise. The Big T riders were pounding up the slope now. He wondered if they would sense his change of direction or go galloping along the main trail.

Tensely he waited in the darkness while another kind of darkness gathered in his mind. He hoped he could stay in the saddle till the Big T crowd raced by. If he fell now, the crash of his fall would carry to them.

The sound of the gelding's labored breathing seemed terribly loud. Then a rolling thunder of hoofs swept up the grade. There was the creak of saddle leather, a rider's indistinguishable yell, then the Big T rushed past.

Corey listened to the racket diminish as the Big T crew hit the top of the grade and plunged swiftly down the far slope. When he could no longer hear any sounds he slid out of the saddle. The brush cushioned his fall. The jolt of the drop sent fresh agony through his side. But it also pushed back the waves of dizziness long enough for him to scramble out of the way of the gelding's hoofs.

Flat on his back, he tore at his shirt, biting back the sob of pain that pushed into his throat. Blood seeped across his fingers. His shirt and undershirt were soaked with it. He found a dry portion of the shirt, however, and managed to rip off a great section of it. Then he wadded it into a thick compress and rammed it into the wound.

149

He knew he ought to get to a creek to bathe it and clean it but he didn't have the strength to move. He couldn't tell how bad it was and could only hope that he would be able to avoid an infection.

The effort of twisting around to fit the compress against the wound took all the starch out of him. The dizziness he had fought off finally overwhelmed him and he lost consciousness.

A gray dawn mist clung to the low brush when he opened his eyes once more. There was a thorough chill in the air. All of his muscles felt congealed. He was numb all over. When he moved, his torn side throbbed with a dull, stiff ache.

For a minute or two he lay in the brush, watching his pony cropping the leaves from a small bush. He lifted a hand to his head. There was a dry heat there that told him he was running a fever. At the same time a chill sent its shuddering impulse through him.

A dismal sense of failure struck him. He'd made a complete mess of everything. Not only had he failed to kill Pole Richmond, he had not gotten the money he'd wanted from Thorpe, and now he had a wound that threatened to smash his entire plan to run away with Ella.

Gritting his teeth in pain, Corey rolled slowly over onto his belly. He got his knees under him, then got up. He staggered over to his horse, wondering bleakly how he was going to heave himself into the saddle. He felt limp and ragged and thoroughly beaten.

Cold sweat seeped out of his forehead while he leaned weakly against the gelding's flanks. He spotted a flat rock nearby. He led the horse over to it. Then, stepping on the rock, he lifted himself into the saddle from that vantage point. He sent the gelding crashing through the brush and back down to the trail.

Once on the trail he angled up the slope to the ridge.

He followed the ridge for a mile, then quartered down a steep, shaly slant to a narrow defile. He rode quickly through the gulch, swung east along the edge of a grassy basin until he reached a small mountain branch.

Dismounting, he hobbled over to the creek. He sank down on his belly, bent his face into the water, and took a long drink. Afterward he sat up, loosened his belt, and drew up his shirt. The crude compress he had wedged against the bullet wound had shifted.

For the first time he had a good look at the tear in his flesh. He saw that the slug had passed right through his side. The wound was not deep, but the lips of it were ragged and quite inflamed. He guessed there was a slight infection. Bathing it in the cold creek water would not help. What he needed was a doctor.

But the nearest doctor was in Two Forks, and he couldn't risk going there. Thorpe would have his men scattered in the hills and in town on the watch for him. He was in no condition to buck them in another gun ruckus. No, town was out. He'd have to see the day through without medical attention. With luck he might get the wound attended to in Dunbar tonight before he and Ella boarded the westbound train.

Meanwhile, there was still the problem of laying his hands on some money. He had nothing at his own ranch. The three silver dollars in his pocket were the full extent of his resources He had to have money. The only place he could get it was at the Big T.

He was reasonably certain that Thorpe, Richmond, and the rest of the Big T crowd would spend most of the day away from the ranch. For one thing, they'd be out looking for him. They would never anticipate his coming back to the ranch. If they all cleared out he could take his own time searching through Thorpe's safe for the money he and Ella would need for a stake. At the same time he could help himself to food. He hadn't eaten for more than twelve hours, and in his weakened condition he needed the energy that food would supply.

Packing the cloth compress against the wound again, Corey stuffed his shirt back into his trousers, tightened his belt, and rose to his feet. Once more he had to lead the gelding over to a flat-topped rock in order to heave his body into the saddle.

Then he rode back to the defile, traversed it at a fast trot, and moved on along the ridge in the direction of Thorpe's ranch.

Half an hour later he sat his horse atop a wooded knoll that overlooked the Big T ranch yard. He was disappointed when he saw a bunch of horses still in the corral and a few of Thorpe's riders dawdling around and swapping yarns in front of the bunkhouse.

He waited for fifteen minutes. When none of the men showed signs of riding off he got out of the saddle, picketed the gelding, and sprawled in the grass to continue his vigil.

Near noon three punchers galloped into the yard. They rode over to the house. Pole Richmond and Guy Thorpe came out of the front room, conferred with the riders a few moments, then went inside again.

Corey wondered if the three men had been part of the bunch detailed to hunt for him. With the three men already lounging in the yard and Thorpe and Richmond in the house, eight of the Big T crew were accounted for. Corey gussed there were another four riders out on the range somewhere. He was surprised that the whole crew wasn't out in the hills or in town, waiting to finish him off.

About one o'clock the three men who had ridden in saddled up fresh horses and went off again. Still the other men lingered. Corey's impatience grew. His wound, too, continued to bother him. There was a steady, throbbing ache in his side. Occasionally he felt dizzy and lightheaded, and he wondered if his fever was rising.

There was a raw, empty sensation in his belly. He couldn't go much longer without eating. Yet he was in no shape to buck all those men in the yard.

Finally, a little after three in the afternoon, Thorpe wandered out of the house, went to the corral, and roped out a horse. Richmond followed a few minutes later and entered the bunkhouse. Then the three men who had been loafing in the yard all morning joined Thorpe at the corral and threw their blankets and rigs on a trio of horses.

Richmond leaned against the doorjamb as Thorpe led his three men out of the yard at a fast run.

Corey watched them go with a hard grin on his mouth. Just one man left. That was a break. And the man was Pole Richmond, the fellow he had missed killing the night before.

Quickly going to his horse, Corey led the animal down the slope through the trees until he was just a few hundred yards from the back wall of the bunkhouse. Then he lifted his gun out of the holster and went forward through the brush. There were two windows in the rear and Corey approached them at an oblique angle, keeping his body at a low crouch. He had his Colt fisted, ready to throw it up for a shot if Richmond spotted him.

He gained the wall without drawing any challenge from inside. Then, flattened against the building, he started his careful circuit of the bunkhouse. As he reached each window he ducked down and crawled past the sill. Once past the rear wall he negotiated the blind side of the building and eased around to the entrance of the bunkhouse.

By that time he was breathing hard from nervousness and exertion. His wounded side punished him with dull twinges of pain. A momentary dizzy spell forced him to lean against the building for support. He shook his head to clear it, glanced quickly toward the main house, then lunged into the open doorway of the bunkhouse.

Richmond had just swung away from a clothing peg on the wall when he saw Corey. Instinctively his right hand dropped toward his gun. But he stopped without any command from Corey when he saw the cocked Colt in Corey's fist.

"I came back to finish my job," Corey said flatly.

Richmond stood still on widespread feet. The pupils of his eyes dilated. There was a savage, trapped look about him.

"Shoot and be damned to you, Corey," he said.

Corey swept his left hand briefly across his eyes. A black mist gathered before him. Richmond's face appeared a little dim and remote. Fear took hold of him. He had to go through this time. He had to get this over with before he blacked out.

"Richmond," he said grimly, "you're a low-down skunk but I'm going to give you a fair shake. When I ram my gun back into leather start your draw."

Richmond's eyes glinted under the brim of his hat. His lips barely moved when he replied. "You damned fool. If I had the drop on you I wouldn't waste any time."

"That's what makes you a polecat," snapped Corey. He drew his arm back. The barrel of his gun raked the top of the holster.

At that instant Richmond's left hand swept his hat off his head and sent it skimming toward Corey. The brim slapped across Corey's cheek as he brought his Colt back into line and fired at the Big T ramrod.

His shot came a split second before Richmond's. The Big T ramrod had made an amazingly fast draw. But he hadn't quite got his barrel lined up when Corey's slug hit him. With a bullet plowing from his gun into the floor at

154

his feet Richmond reeled and went down. Just before he struck the boards Corey got a glimpse of a broad red splash of blood seeping down across his face from the top of his skull.

Corey didn't wait to see any more. The job was done. Suddenly he found no pleasure in it. Sickness worried the pit of his stomach. The dizziness whirled back in front of his eyes and he had to stir himself to keep from falling.

He wheeled from the bunkhouse doorway and hurried to the main house. Every step set the trip hammer beating in his head and side. But he kept on. He had to get his hands on some money. He didn't know how much time he had. Thorpe or some of the others might be coming back soon. If they caught him here he'd wind up in boot-hill.

Frantically Corey stumbled up the veranda steps. He charged into the front room and headed straight for the iron safe against the far wall. Kneeling down in front of the safe, he started to fumble with the combination. He wasted five minutes at the dial but had no success.

With a curse he got up, retreated a few steps. He drew his gun, took careful aim at the lock, and let go with a shot. The bullet smashed against the hard metal, denting it, then ricocheted across the room. Twice more he fired at the lock. But it held firm.

He wheeled away from the safe, hurried to the window. A glance out across the flats showed no sign of horsemen. But the emptiness of the terrain brought him no relief. He moved over to the desk. He tugged at the closed roll-top. It refused to budge. It, too, was locked.

Corey pulled out his Colt again, fired one shot at the frail lock that held the top to the flat base of the desk. Wood chips sprayed outward from the region of the lock as the slug ripped through the top and on inside.

He rolled the top back and found himself faced with a row of cluttered pigeonholes. Hurriedly he groped through the scattered assortment of papers in the various racks. As he emptied each compartment he flung the papers on the floor. At last he came to a battered leather wallet stuffed under some old tally books. Inside the wallet he found five hundred dollars in bills. He pulled the money out of the wallet, folded it up, and shoved it into his pocket.

Little as the sum was, he realized it would have to do. He had no time for additional searching. The afternoon was waning and he still had a long ride ahead of him to meet Ella at the abandoned line shack.

15   From the moment she got up that morning Ella was nervous. The long hours of the day seemed to stretch endlessly ahead of her. She didn't know how she'd be able to wait until the time of her meeting with Corey.

Ella was thankful for one thing. Winston hadn't come home. He had ridden into Two Forks the night before on business and had informed Ella he meant to stay over in the hotel. She had no idea when he would return to the ranch, but she hoped that he would join the crew out on the range without stopping off to see her. She actually dreaded seeing him again.

But even as the thought of Winston ran through her mind she saw him ride into the yard. The crew had long since gone off. From the wide window in the front room she saw him dismount in front of the veranda, loop the reins of his horse around the hitching rail, then come stamping up the steps.

She turned as he shouldered into the room.

"Hello, Van," she said.

"Did you miss me?" he asked with the queer, taunting rasp that had been in his voice since their first night together. It was as if he thoroughly understood her feelings about him and took a sadistic delight in letting her know he meant to make her live up to the letter of her bargain.

Ella didn't answer the question. She let herself be drawn into his arms. She tried not to recoil when his mouth bruised her lips in a rough kiss. He was hard and quick and gluttonous in everything he did. He had a way of snatching at the things in life—taking them by force by the sheer drive of his will. He was that way in his love-making. When he finally released her he looked her up and down as if she were a prime steer he was appraising for the beef market.

"Ella, you're worth coming home to," he said. Then he gave her a sly, amused glance. "That hotel idea last night wasn't so good."

"Why?" Ella asked. "Didn't you sleep well?"

She could have bitten off her tongue the moment she spoke. Too late she realized what was coming.

"It wasn't that at all," he said. "But a freshly married man ought to spend his evenings at home with his wife. What do you think?"

Ella's voice toned upward. "I didn't mind, Van."

Swiftly the amusement washed out of his eyes. In its place slid something dark and ugly. "Why don't you say what you really mean?" he demanded curtly.

"I don't understand you," she said, coloring under his intent, probing gaze.

"Hell, you were damned glad you didn't have to sleep with me last night."

He pulled her close. Fear crawled through Ella like a slimy, unclean thing. She couldn't trust herself to answer him. He had hit upon the true state of her feelings with terrifying exactness. Her silence lent impetus to his gathering rage and suspicion.

"Where did you go yesterday afternoon?" Winston asked.

The question caught Ella unawares. A tremor of emotion shook her. She said tightly, "Just for a ride."

"Meet anybody you know?"

Ella paused a fraction of a second before saying, "No."

"That's a damned lie!" Winston's hands fastened like steel bands around Ella's arms. "You were out seeing Tom Frazer!"

"It's not true!" Ella protested.

"Don't tell me. That's the only reason why you'd go riding."

For a moment Ella thought she had been seen meeting Corey at the line shack. But linking her name again with Tom's showed that Winston was just giving voice to his old suspicions.

"Let me go," she pleaded. "You're hurting me."

Winston's eyes flashed. There was no mercy in him. "This is nothing compared to what will happen if you don't stay away from Frazer."

Suddenly Ella's pent-up emotions gave way. She wrenched half out of Winston's grasp. Then she swung the flat of her hand against his cheek. The blow stung the rancher. He let go of her other arm. With a deliberate savagery he slapped her face first on one side, then on the other. The force of those slaps rocked Ella backward. The back of her knees struck the edge of a chair. She fell into it, cowering away from him. One hand crept to her burning cheek where the imprint of Winston's fingers lay like ruddy welts.

"Get this, Ella," Winston said. "I'm running this ranch and I'm running you. You'll take orders like anybody in my crew. Hereafter when you go riding you'll have company. One of the hands will ride with you."

Ella said nothing. She crouched in the chair, feeling bruised and beaten. Winston's threat to keep her from riding alone promised to ruin everything. An odd dryness filled her mouth and throat. She had difficulty in swallowing.

Hoofbeats drummed loudly in the yard. Ella sat up, brushing a hand across her eyes. Boots thumped across the veranda. Jess Engel, the Circle W foreman, walked in.

"I've got the crew working the south range, Van. Do you still want to take a look at the grass up in that northeast section?"

"Yeah. But you stay here."

"What'll I do here?" Engel asked, frowning in surprise.

Winston jerked his head at Ella. "Now that I've got a wife, Jess," he said with an odd intonation, "I don't like to leave her on the ranch alone."

Engel looked at Ella and grinned. Ella turned her face away.

"I reckon I know how it is, Van," the foreman told him. "I'll be glad to keep an eye on her."

"Good," said Winston. "I'll have a look at that northeast section myself. And if Ella feels like going riding this afternoon you tag along. The range isn't as safe for riding as it used to be."

Engel grinned knowingly. "I reckon you're right, Van."

Winston turned to look at Ella. She met his stare with a bright, hard anger that tugged a low laugh from him. She loathed the sight of him now. His eyes, so possessive and arrogant in the way they traveled over her, made her flesh crawl.

Then, because he knew she'd have to act a part in front of Engel, he moved over to her and deliberately kissed her again. Afterward he followed Engel out the door and both men vanished around the side of the house, going toward the corral.

Ella didn't move from the chair until she heard Winston rush away from the ranch at a fast gallop. Then she rose stiffly and walked down the hall to the kitchen. She glanced out into the rear yeard. Engel was perched atop

160

the corral fence, whittling at a stick with a sharp-bladed knife. The foreman had taken up his position as sentry.

Ella's nervousness grew by leaps and bounds. If Engel stayed in the yard she would have no opportunity to slip away from the ranch. She needed a horse to make her escape, and it was clear that Engel meant to stay within sight of the corral and barn.

Wearily Ella went back to the hall and up the stairs to the second floor. In the roughly furnished bedroom she shared with Winston she went to a clothes closet and brought out a small valise. From a bureau drawer she took a small pile of underclothes and crammed them into the suitcase. The few dresses and skirts she owned also went into the valise. She closed the lid, flipped the catches, and left the valise on the bed.

She was prepared to run. But only time would tell if she could get safely away. Each time she went to the window to look down into the rear yard she saw that Engel was still there. He had moved to the wooden bench in front of the bunkhouse. The changed position, however, still gave him full command of the house and the corral.

At noontime Ella made a light lunch for herself. She ate little. Nervousness had taken away her appetite. The early afternoon dragged on. Engel still maintained his vigil by the bunkhouse.

Ella grew frantic. If there were only some way she could lure the foreman from his sentry post. Several plans occurred to her. Each had to be discarded as hopeless. Then, going to the small dark pantry where flour and other food staples were stored to put away a tin of coffee, a new idea came to her mind. She saw how she might be able to immobilize the ramrod for a brief period.

Hurrying to the back door, she called the foreman. "Jess, can you come here for a moment?"

Engel rose from the bench and said, "Sure thing."

161

He put down the old saddle he had been mending and sauntered through the gray dust of the yard to the back door. His dark-skinned, dour face surveyed Ella boldly when he stepped past her into the kitchen.

"What can I do for you?" he asked.

Ella disliked the man intensely. He was of the same breed as Winston—arrogant and ruthless and careless of the feelings of others. But now she showéd him a friendly smile. She gestured to the dark, windowless pantry.

"There's a big bag of flour on one of the lower shelves in there," she said. "Would you mind getting it for me?"

Engel stared at her in surprise. "You figuring on doing some baking?" He grinned. "That's supposed to be Mrs. Loring's job. She's the cook and housekeeper."

"I'm well aware of that. But Van gave her a few days off to visit some relatives over in Dunbar. So, if you don't mind, I'd like that flour."

Ella felt the blood rush to her cheeks under Engel's sharp scrutiny. All of her muscles seemed to be freezing up with the sudden tension that assailed her. She moistened her dry lips with her tongue.

The Circle W ramrod shrugged. "All right, Ella," he said with blunt familiarity. "Some biscuits would go good for supper."

Ella retreated a step to let Engel walk in front of her. When he entered the gloomy pantry she was right at his heels. "There it is," she said. "Toward the back."

He blundered into the storage room, slamming one big hip against a shelf. Immediately Ella swung the door shut and twisted the key in the lock.

"Damn it, Ella! What are you doing?" Engel yelled, his voice muffled as it seeped through the wooden panel of the door.

"That's obvious, isn't it?" she retorted. "I'm locking you in for a while."

162

"Let me out or I'll bust the door down!" Engel threatened.

Ella, her heart pumping rapidly, now that the ruse had worked, hurried upstairs for the packed valise. By the time she returned to the kitchen the ramrod was banging heavily against the door.

"Ella!" he shouted. "Let me out of here!"

She didn't answer his cry. But in a pause between his yells he heard her go past the pantry. He threw himself against the door, rattling the hinges and shaking the entire room. Ella saw the way the frail panels bellied out under the thrust of the foreman's brawny shoulders and realized the door would not withstand much of a battering.

With a nervous gasp of breath she dashed out into the yard. There were a half-dozen horses prancing about in the corral. She raced into the barn for a rope, made a loop, and prepared to catch her favorite mare. From the house she heard a booming that told of Engel's savage efforts to escape. A terrible frenzy gripped her. She should have had the foreman saddle the mare for her on the pretext of going for a ride. Now she had to waste precious minutes roping the horse and getting the rig in place.

Luck smiled at her when the mare, sighting her, whinnied and trotted close. The first cast of the rope was successful. Ella gently drew the animal toward the fence, looped the rope around a post until she got a blanket and saddle.

She had the saddle cinched in place and was leading the mare through the open gate when a splintering crash of wood warned her that Engel was breaking down the pantry door.

With the valise in one hand, she put a foot into the stirrup and climbed to the saddle. Then she spurred the mare back into the corral. A shrill cry spilled from her throat as she raced the mare at the other animals in the enclosure. She caught one gelding on the rump with the snapping end of her reins. The gelding bolted, crashed into a mare. In a second all of the horses in the corral headed toward the open gate. Ella followed close behind them, whipping them on and yelling at the top of her voice.

As the horses sped across the ranch yard Jess Engel reeled through the back door.

"Ella! Come back here!" he roared.

"Not today, Jess!" she called. "Tell Van so long for me."

Engel made a lunge for one of the geldings bolting past him. He missed the animal and went down in the dust. Then the herd was past him and running hard. He got up, shouted at Ella to stop.

The girl paid no heed. She heard the flat crack of a gun. Twisting in the saddle, she saw smoke dribbling from the barrel of the ramrod's .45. The shot was a warning. Engel was accurate with a Colt. He dropped to one knee in the dust and his arm straightened out. Ella knew Engel wouldn't dare shoot at her. But he wouldn't hesitate to bring down the mare.

Frantic with dread, Ella ripped out her own .38. She hadn't done much shooting with it. Her hand shook with nervousness. But she brought up the weapon, snapped a shot at Engel, and was amazed to see his Colt drop from his hand. He fell on top of it, writhing in the dust.

16   The sight of Engel going down sickened Ella. The .38 slipped from her fingers. Her blood turned to ice at the thought that Engel might be dying. She turned in the saddle for another look at him. He was sprawled out flat in the dust, not moving now. The mare galloped on, carrying Ella farther out of range.

As she raced toward the hills a dull presentiment of evil rippled through her. The still, hot afternoon throbbed with a silent threat of disaster. She couldn't tell why this was so. There seemed to be a heavy pressure all around her. It was inside her, too, lashing her nerves into knots.

This was a bad beginning. The memory of Engel's flattened-out shape came back to haunt her. Despair moved in, dragging her spirits down. She was leaving her husband for another man. And Winston, vengeful devil that he was, would scour the ends of the earth looking for her and Corey. Even if she and Corey got safely away, each day in the future would be lived on borrowed time. Time borrowed from certain death.

Ella never remembered much of the long ride to the abandoned line cabin in the hills. Every mile she traveled the fear of pursuit rode with her. Also, she dreaded meeting anyone on the trail. Only once did she sight a small party of horsemen. She detoured through a thick patch of brush to avoid them and returned to the trail a good two miles beyond them.

Though she pushed the mare at a rapid pace she did not reach the line shack until a scant half-hour before dusk. The open glade in front of the cabin was already bathed in a cool half-light when she saw Corey step out of the trees beside the cabin, leading his horse.

"I thought you weren't coming," Corey said.

"I had some trouble," Ella told him as she got down, letting the valise slide to the ground.

Corey came over to her, his face intense. "Were you followed?"

"I—I don't think so."

"You've got to be sure."

"I'm as sure as I can be." Ella saw the haggard, strained look on Corey's face. Then as her glance shifted along his muscular frame she saw the dark, telltale stain on the side of his shirt. "Bill, you've been shot!"

"Just a flesh wound," he said. "It'll be all right."

"But your eyes," she said. "They look feverish. Let me see the wound. Maybe I can fix it up."

"No. There's no time. I'll let the sawbones in Dunbar fix it up."

Ella's mouth tightened with strain. She didn't like Corey's ruddy complexion. He was running a fever. That meant an infection. "Bill," she said, "maybe you oughtn't wait too long. If there's an infection it might——"

Corey shook his head impatiently. "Ella, I'll have to take my chances. We can't risk going into Two Forks. I reckon some dirt got into the wound, but it's not too bad."

"How did it happen, Bill?"

"I had a run-in with Thorpe's bunch when I went up there to get some money."

Worry pinched Ella's features. "Did you get any money?"

"Yeah. But I had to help myself." Swiftly he outlined the events that had occurred at the Big T ranch.

Ella clung to Corey. All her dependence was on him now. "Why did you take such a chance?"

"I had to go back for money. Without that we couldn't even get out of Dunbar. Besides, it gave me another shot at Pole Richmond."

"He might have killed you."

"But he didn't." Corey's face set in gray, ridged lines. "He had a killing coming to him for beating up Tom and sending him to his death."

A sudden shiver ran through Ella. Her eyes widened with shock. "Tom dead? He—he can't be." Frazer no longer meant anything emotionally to her, yet somehow she couldn't conceive of him being dead.

Corey's eyes brimmed over with bitterness. The memory of Tom Frazer would stay with him all his days. He blamed himself for the fate that had overtaken Tom. If he hadn't run with Thorpe's wild bunch Tom might be alive. They could have seen things through together. That's the way it should have been. Only he—Bill Corey—hadn't had guts enough to live like a man.

"I reckon Tom is gone all right," he told Ella. "He spotted some rustled Double-Y cows up in the hills and ran into some of Thorpe's bunch on the way to re-brand the critters. They chased him to the river. He got away in an old rowboat but was swept over the falls."

"Oh, my God!" Ella gasped. "Poor Tom." She felt a deep pang of regret inside her. There wasn't a better man in all the range than Tom Frazer. She'd given him shabby treatment. And now he was dead. "If he'd only had some help," she said.

"I know," said Corey grimly. "That's what devils me.

167

He played a lone hand. I could have helped him—but I didn't."

Ella looked at him, her eyes shadowed and intent. "How do you know so much about what happened? Have you been running with Thorpe's bunch?"

He smiled thinly. "Would it make any difference?"

Ella watched him. He was her only salvation. She loved him as much as she could love any man. She guessed now how he got his money. He rustled other men's cows. The chances were he had helped to steal Double-Y cows. That was why he'd gone to Thorpe for money. But in this desperate hour of need she didn't care.

"No, Bill," she said. "It doesn't make any difference. We're two of a kind, I guess. We're renegades. We're both taking what doesn't belong to us. You killed Richmond to get away. And I—I killed Jess Engel!" Her voice rose, then trembled on the edge of panic.

Corey straightened in rigid stupefaction. "You killed Engel? How did you come to do that?"

Ella gripped Corey's shirt front with trembling hands. "Winston has been suspicious of me right along. He found out I went riding yesterday. He thinks I went to meet Tom. This morning when he returned from an overnight trip to town he ordered Engel to stay around to keep a watch on me. If I went riding, Engel was to tag along."

She paused, suppressed a shudder of black memory, then went on. "It got later and later. I was afraid I wouldn't be able to meet you. Engel stayed in the yard where he could watch the house. Finally I called him into the house, asked him to get a bag of flour from the pantry. The moment he stepped into the pantry I slammed the door and locked him in."

"But I don't see how——"

Ella interrupted Corey. "He broke the door down. By the time I got the mare saddled and hazed the remaining horses out of the corral Engel had gotten free. As I rode across the yard he fired one warning shot. I saw he meant to bring down the mare. I—I couldn't help myself. I fired at him with my .38. He went down." A sob caught in her throat. Tears stung her eyes. "When I—I looked back at him he wasn't moving at all."

"Good Lord!" breathed Corey, holding her. "We've sure played hell. I don't wonder you're upset."

Ella's body shook, and she clung to him fiercely. "Oh, Bill, I've a feeling this isn't going to work out. Everything's going wrong."

Corey's teeth clicked together. Fever churned in his head. His eyelids felt weighted and heavy. But out of some stubborn reserve of strength he drew a stern reply. "Don't talk that way, Ella. We've burned our bridges. It's too late for regrets. We've got to run." He stared up at the sky, fast turning pink in the west. "Time to move. When Winston finds you gone he'll fill every trail with riders looking for you."

"He'll try the Double-Y first," Ella said.

"And after that, if he's as smart as I think he is, he'll head for railhead at Dunbar."

Fear goaded Ella with cruel spurs. "Bill," she asked, "do you think we'll make it?"

Corey answered out of a dismal weariness. "I'm not worried about reaching Dunbar," he said. "I'm worried about how long it will take Winston to figure the play correctly."

He walked unsteadily back to his horse. He put a foot into the stirrup, tried to heave himself into the saddle, but fell back. To keep from slipping to the ground he grabbed the gelding's rump.

Ella rushed up to him. "Bill, you're hurt bad!" Dread was a black, insidious poison in her. "You can't ride."

"I've got to," he said grimly, sweat standing out in cold

169

beads on his sun-browned forehead. "Just give me a hand up."

Ella nodded mutely. Her eyes were smoky. She kept staring back down the trail she had followed. Any moment she expected the woods to disgorge a column of Circle W riders. Corey thrust his left boot in the stirrup. Ella cupped her slender hands under his right boot and shoved upward with all her strength. This time Corey made it. But when he hit the saddle blackness swam sluggishly before his eyes and he had to clutch at the horn to keep his balance.

"Bill, are you sure you can make it?" Ella asked gravely.

Angry at his own weakness, Corey snapped at her. "Leave me alone and get on your horse."

Ella's features twisted in sudden hurt. Quietly she returned to the mare, mounted, and joined him in a quick run from the clearing.

Corey set a hard pace for them. It took its toll of him though he tried to hide his suffering from Ella. Every stride of the gelding sent its individual jolt through his body. More than once he gripped the saddle horn as dizziness swirled over him. At times he lost all concept of his surroundings. He was aware only of a steady pounding inside him. The long minutes stretched out into black infinity, and it seemed that he and Ella had been riding forever.

Darkness overtook them when they were still three miles from Corey's two-bit spread. Corey's horse, given its head, slowed to a canter. Ella pulled in her mare to stay abreast of Corey. She watched him with a straining anxiety. He was traveling on sheer nerve. How long could he continue? She dared not risk a guess.

Suddenly they drifted into the ranch yard. The gelding halted near the back door. Ella slid down from the mare at once. She hurried to Corey. He eased from the saddle, half fell against her, then steadied himself along the house wall. A great, ragged sigh spilled from his lungs. A warm wetness crawling down his side told him that the wound had opened and was bleeding again.

Ella's arms circled his waist. "Bill, you can't go on this way. Get inside and lie down. You need a doctor."

He whirled on her angrily. "No, damn it!" He brushed a hand across his tired eyes. "We can't risk that. If we're caught I'm done. Don't you understand that?" He moved along the house wall to the rear door. "We'll take the buckboard. It'll be slower, but I—I can't stand that saddle any more."

Ella helped Corey inside the littered back room that served as a kitchen. She lit a lamp. Corey sagged into a chair, dropped his arms on the scrubbed wooden table. "There's a bottle of whisky on the shelf. Bring it here," he said.

Ella found the bottle. It was half full. She pulled the cork, handed it to him. He grabbed it, locked his lips around the neck of the bottle, and took a deep draught. Afterward he set it down on the table. Heat spread upward through his vitals. His head cleared. He got up, went to a corner of the room, and picked up his few belongings wrapped in a tight bedroll.

"You want to go now?" Ella asked.

"The westbound leaves Dunbar at nine," he said. "That doesn't give us too much time. Come out to the barn. I'll need your help hitching the team of grays to the wagon."

Ella took the lamp out to the barn. Together they got the buckboard ready. Ella threw her valise into the bed of the wagon beside Corey's bedroll. Then they climbed to the seat and clattered out of the yard.

Night swallowed them once they struck the wagon road. Wind came out of the west, gently scented with

171

sage. Stars wheeled in frosty brilliance through the sky's black vault. Trees whipped by in a dark, formless blur. The road dipped up and down with the shifting contours of the country. They crossed a shallow creek, the iron-tired wheels striking sharp echoes from the rocks of the ford. Then the road pitched upward toward a wide bench that ran north for two miles before veering to the west.

On their right loomed the heavy bulk of a high, shaly bluff. The road narrowed, skirting the cliff base. Off to the left, in a slanting line, a shoulder of loose earth dropped in a steep slope to a culvert that carried flood waters during the spring and fall rains.

Suddenly over the racket of the grays' pounding hoofs they heard a muted thunder.

"What's that?" Ella demanded.

There was an abrupt smell of dust in the air. A loose rock bounded across the road. Another glanced off the side of the buckboard. The rumble of sound was nearer now, seemingly above them.

Corey's cheeks turned chalky. Raw fear howled through him.

"It's a slide!" he yelled. "Hold on. We'll have to make a run for it!"

He grabbed the whip, laid the stinging tip of it on the grays. The wagon lurched as the team leaned into the traces. A booming roar filled the night. Dust rose in a cloud around them. A few more rocks cascaded down the slope to the road. Then in a great rush of sound an avalanche of loose dust and stones hurtled down the slope and swept over the wagon.

Ella screamed once. Then even that shrill cry was silenced in the wild racket. The slide, moving like a terrible Frankenstein, swooped down upon the buckboard and its occupants. There was a great rending and tearing of wood, then utter fogged stillness.

172

17   Frazer rode swiftly under the bland night sky. The yellow stain of brilliance from the Double-Y ranch lights dropped out of sight beyond a swell of ground. Although weariness still lay in all his bones and the need for sleep was a demand he could not long deny, he felt reasonably capable of seeing the night through.

The meal Margo had given him together with the few drinks of brandy he had consumed had been a marvelous pickup. He had also taken the time for a quick dip in the creek pool several hundred yards behind the house. Afterward he had changed into fresh clothes, gotten a spare six-gun out of his bedroll, and thrown his riding gear on the back of a rangy, long-gaited sorrel gelding.

The horse liked to run, and he gave it full rein. There was a lot to be done this night before the posse he hoped to recruit could get back into the hills. He was a little worried about the day now gone. If Thorpe had any doubts at all about his dying in the plunge over the brink of the falls he would have wasted no time in shifting the stolen beef. In that event the posse would have its work cut out for it, hunting the critters and catching the Big T crew with them. However, there was nothing else to be done. The chance had to be taken. The cattle were up there and he didn't think Thorpe would move them over the state line without first re-branding them and waiting a few weeks for the scars to heal.

After a fast ten-minute run Frazer pulled the sorrel in to a ground-eating canter. He had a lot of riding ahead of him and he didn't want to run the risk of the animal foundering on him in the hills.

Five miles from the Double-Y ranch the trail he was following cut into the main wagon road to the county seat at Dunbar. Since Sam Bassett's Pothook outfit was situated a few miles northwest of his present position Frazer decided to use the road.

He had splashed through the rocky ford of a creek and was negotiating the twisting grade beyond when a dull, booming thunder was telegraphed to him by the brisk wind. For a moment he glanced toward the sky, looking for the massed clouds in the west that would herald the approach of a storm. But the heavens were clear and star-dappled.

The sound came to him again, this time in a long, echoing reverberation. Suddenly he placed the racket as coming from a point two miles ahead of him where the wagon road skirted a shaly bluff.

He drew to a halt. The sound swelled to a great roar, then gradually dwindled away. Silence clamped a lid once more on the night. He knew, then, that somewhere ahead of him another slide of rock and earth had come cascading down the cliff to swarm across the road. The chances were that the road was blocked and he'd have to detour through the thick brush to reach the Pothook ranch.

Yet some faint premonition of disaster he could not explain impelled him to ride on to investigate the scene of the landslide. He spurred the gelding up the hill. Once on top of the bench the sorrel stretched its legs and went streaking across country.

Within a mile Frazer detected the odor of freshly dis-

174

turbed dust. Off ahead through the trees the low night sky was fogged with a slowly rising pall of gray dust. The scent of that dust grew heavier and more pronounced with every stride the sorrel took.

Galloping around a point of rock, Frazer came suddenly upon a great mound of dirt and rubble that barricaded the entire width of the road. Through the fog of dust he saw something else that brought a swift stab of fear to him.

Half-buried in that swarm of loose shale and rock were the shattered, broken remains of a buckboard. Beyond the wagon just the head of a horse was visible. The animal seemed to be dead. Its mate, caught in a tangle of harness and partially trapped by debris, was struggling to free itself, whinnying in terror all the while.

Frazer jumped down from the sorrel and ran forward. He reached the great hill of earth that covered the road. His boots slipped and slid in the loose shale, but he clambered toward the downed horses. Then, just a few yards to his left near the edge of a culvert, he saw a dim, huddled shape. He stopped, pivoted in that direction. A few steps took him to Ella. Only her face and upper body were visible. The rest of her was covered by broken rubble from the cliff.

He dropped down beside her. "Ella! Ella!" he cried. There was no answer. He bent closer. Fearfully he placed a hand upon her breast. He expected to find no movement there, but was amazed when he felt her heart pumping slowly beneath the pressure of his palm.

A jagged, rough-edged sigh of relief escaped from him. He fumbled for a packet of matches. He found one at last. He scratched the sulphur tip against a stone. In the guttering yellow light cupped in his palms he examined Ella. There was a cruel red gash over her ear. Blood streaked her hair and stained her cheek. Her skin was a sickly white color. There was a bruise high in the center of her forehead.

The match burned down to his fingertips and flickered out. Frazer tossed it away. Then he stooped to the rubble and began clearing it away from Ella's body with his bare hands. In a few minutes he had freed her legs. He examined them cursorily, exploring for broken bones. He found nothing to indicate a break. But there still remained the very real danger that she might be suffering from internal injuries.

He gathered her body gently in his arms and carried her down from the pile of earth and rocks. Once in the road he set her down, debating his next move. He had to get her to a doctor but he couldn't risk taking her on his saddle. If she had internal injuries it would be the worst thing he could do. He needed a wagon. The nearest place he could get one was the Pothook outfit.

Then, moving along the edge of the road where the earth was not piled so high, he almost stumbled over a torn open valise. It was filled with feminine clothes. He knew at once they were Ella's. And her presence on the Dunbar road at this hour of the night told him something else. She was running away. There could be no other explanation. And with that thought came another even more disturbing.

Corey hadn't been able to leave Ella alone. Her marriage to Van Winston hadn't changed anything between them. They still wanted each other. Frazer remembered now with startling clarity how he had come upon them at the abandoned line shack.

Suddenly he was sure that Corey was here, somewhere in the wreckage of the wagon. Ella wasn't the type to pull up stakes and go it alone. If she was running, there'd be another man. The man had to be Corey.

With a dull, dreary sense of despair Frazer painted the

176

grim scene of Ella's and Corey's flight. They'd arranged to meet somewhere in the late afternoon—probably at the line shack—then had gone on to Corey's place to pick up the buckboard. The fact that they were on the Dunbar road could mean only one thing. They had intentions of taking the nine-o'clock westbound train.

Though he knew Ella needed immediate attention, Frazer couldn't go off without searching through the rubble for Corey. He didn't have much hope. Still he had to look. He moved across the loose earth, lifting aside big rocks, pawing through the shale and dirt. He went around to the smashed buckboard. Broken boards stuck up out of the debris like the shattered spars of a derelict ship. He tugged them free. He used one jagged-edged board to root through the dirt. Every lunge of that makeshift spade left him in a cold sweat as he waited, trembling, for the shock of the wood striking the yielding, torn flesh of his friend.

He spent fifteen minutes in that frantic search and found nothing. His arms ached from digging. Perspiration bathed his armpits, trickled down his back and sides. If Corey was here, he was buried deep beneath the slide.

The certainty of Corey's doom settled like a cold stone in Frazer's stomach. Wild and weak and mercurial as Corey had been, there had been a firm attachment between the two men that nothing could sever. They'd had good times together. It didn't matter that Corey had done the one thing that would forever ostracize him from Two Forks. Women held a sacred place in the West. To take another man's wife was to ask for quick and violent retribution. Corey had gone over the deep end tonight. He had taken the step that put him beyond the pale—and now he was dead.

It was better than a bullet or a hang noose, Frazer told himself. Yet Corey's going would leave a vast empty place in Frazer that nothing could fill—neither time nor the love of a woman.

He had decided to abandon the search and was scrambling back to Ella when he heard the racket of a fast-traveling bunch of horsemen. As he waited for them to appear around the point of rock the moon shot up out of a bank of clouds low in the west. Instantly the grim havoc wrought by the landslide was brought into bold relief by the bright shafts of moonlight.

There was a wind-whipped shout from the still-unseen column, the hard clatter of iron-shod hoofs, then the riders sped into view coming at a fast run. The two men in the lead saw the piled-up rubble that blocked the road and sent their mounts skidding to a halt.

"Who's that?" Van Winston's peremptory voice queried. "Sing out!" Behind him a dozen cowhands drew to a halt with a creak of saddle leather and the jangle of bit chains.

"All right, Van," said Frazer. "It's Frazer."

"By God, look at that slide!" exclaimed the rider next to Winston. "There's a wagon too. Yours, Frazer?"

Frazer shook his head, watching Winston as the latter pushed his mount forward. "No. But Ella—your wife—is here," he said directly to the Circle W owner. "She's pretty badly hurt."

Winston exploded into quick wrath. "You damned skunk. I knew it!" His gun snaked into his hand in a draw hidden by the closeness of the rider beside him. "Keep your dewclaws away from your cutter. This is the end of the line for you!"

Frazer debated going for his Colt. But all down the line he saw silvery moonlight glinting on the barrels of six-guns. Any overt move on his part now would be suicidal.

"Adams," said Winston to the rider beside him, "get Frazer's gun. And be careful. We'll cover you."

The puncher climbed down from his horse. He moved warily up to Frazer. He jerked Frazer's Colt from his holster, then leaped back out of reach. He tossed it over to Winston. The rancher caught it and shoved the weapon into the waistband of his trousers.

"Three or four of you, get down and come with me," he said to the crew behind him.

The nearest punchers complied with the order. The rest spread out across the road, their manner tense and alert.

Winston strode heavily up to Frazer. He stopped within a foot of the ramrod. "You had your warning to stay away from Ella. You're through now, damn you." He swung a fist at Frazer. Frazer side-stepped, but the blow caught him along the side of his head and knocked him off his feet.

By the time Frazer rose again Winston had hurried past him and was kneeling beside the motionless figure of his wife. Two of the Circle W punchers followed him. The rest formed a ring around Frazer. There was a wicked shine in their eyes. They were braced for violence. Frazer saw that he had to take whatever was dished out to him. He had no alternative.

But he spoke to Winston's back. "It's not like you think, Van."

Winston straightened up. His shoulders twitched beneath his black coat. His big hands knotted into fists. "Like hell it isn't. You talked Ella into running away and this is the result."

"No, Van."

"Shut up!" grated Winston. "There's all the proof I need." He pointed to the smashed suitcase from which torn remnants of Ella's clothes protruded. "I've been suspicious of you two right along. Today I left Jess Engel back at the ranch to keep an eye on things. Ella made a run for it late this afternoon. When Engel tried to stop

179

her she put a bullet through his shoulder. She was on her way to meet you."

Frazer stood immobile. He watched one of Winston's riders free the trapped horse from the tangled harness. The animal snorted and trotted off into the nearby trees. As Frazer swung his attention back to his captor he became conscious of the solid wall of hostility that enclosed him. All of these men had him pegged for one of the lowest crimes known to the West. He was worse than a horse thief or a rustler. As such, they would not hesitate to put a bullet in him.

"You've got to listen to me," he said. "I was riding over to see Bassett at the Pothook about——" He broke off momentarily, not wishing to reveal to these men the purpose of his mission. Before he could go on Winston cut in.

"Yeah, you were riding to the Pothook and you heard the roar of the slide so you put your horse to a gallop. When you got here you found Ella lying unconscious."

There was a corrosive scorn in Winston's tone and his eyes held a black, outraged glitter. Frazer met Winston's gaze levelly.

"That's the way it was," he stated. "She was half-buried in dirt and rocks. I had to dig her out."

Even as he spoke Frazer saw the cold disbelief in Winston's face. And he had to admit to himself that his story sounded thin. Yet he could not bring himself to name Bill Corey. Though he was sure that Corey was submerged somewhere in the rubble he could not take refuge in his friend. Better to let Winston hear the truth from Ella when she regained consciousness.

But a look at her white, immobile features filled him with a slowly mounting fear that she might even now be dying. And in dying she would carry the real story of this night's events with her.

180

Suddenly Winston's harsh voice broke into his somber reverie. "Adams, take a run over to the Pothook. Get a buckboard and don't take no for an answer. We've got to get Ella into town to Doc Marlow and we can't risk carrying her on horseback."

The puncher ran back to his horse, mounted quickly. "How will we get the damned wagon around this rubble? I'll never be able to drive through the brush."

Winston's answer was crisp and precise. "Take the old cutoff on your way back. It meets the Twin Forks road about three miles from here. Then you can strike back in this direction through the arroyo that winds up near this point of rock."

Adams nodded in understanding, then pushed his mount down the shaly slope to the culvert. He rode carefully around the slide tailings, quartered up the slope again, and struck off at a fast clip down the road.

After Adams had gone Winston went back to Ella. He knelt beside her, loosened the shirt around her neck. He sent one of the other punchers off to a nearby creek for a hatful of water. When the man came back Winston took off his bandanna, soaked it in the water, and proceeded to bathe Ella's face. But his ministrations were of no avail in bringing her back to consciousness. Finally, with a violent oath, he lurched to his feet.

Frazer looked at Winston, then at the still form of the girl. She appeared so frail and helpless lying in the road. There was no telling how seriously she was injured. She might be suffering from a concussion or a skull fracture. If the latter were the case, even this delay of waiting for the wagon might prove fatal.

Winston tramped over to Frazer. "God help you, Frazer, if Ella dies," he grated.

"I want her well as much as you do," Frazer told him.

Winston's eyes were like burning brands. "You won't be here to see her live or die," he said.

"What are you going to do with him?" one of the Circle W crew asked Winston.

Before the rancher could reply another man cut in, "Hell, there's only one answer to that. String him up. There are plenty of trees around here for that."

"Now you're talking!" shouted a third man.

The cry was taken up, and the men on horseback crowded forward. One of them yelled, "Here's my lass rope, Van."

Frazer felt the solid wash of evil flow against him. These men were in a killing mood. One word from Winston would set them off like the fuse on a stick of dynamite. Frazer felt his blood run thick and cold in his veins. He was not afraid of dying. Give him a gun or a rifle or even a knife and he'd take his chances in any crowd. But a rope around the neck with no opportunity to fight back was another matter.

"We'll take care of that in town," said Winston. "I want him to hang where everyone can see him."

"What about the sheriff?" asked a Circle W puncher.

"I'll handle him." Winston gestured to the man who had just spoken and added: "Take some pigging string and tie Frazer's hands behind his back."

The puncher explored through his pants pockets and came up with several lengths of thin rawhide. While Winston held a gun on him Frazer had to submit to having his wrists firmly bound together behind his back.

After that the group settled down impatiently to wait for Adams to return from the Pothook with a buckboard.

18 An hour later the grim Circle W cavalcade rolled into Two Forks. A mile outside of town Winston had sent a couple of riders ahead of the column to alert the doctor. But Frazer, seeing a small huddle of men gathered in the middle of the dusty street, knew that the Circle W messengers had also seen to it that news of his capture and proposed hanging was thoroughly circulated among the saloons.

"Stand aside!" Winston ordered stridently as the curious onlookers converged on the party, intent on seeing Frazer as well as Ella.

The mob retreated grudgingly. The driver of the buckboard wheeled the vehicle on down the street and pulled up in front of the rotted frame building that housed Doc Marlow's office and living quarters.

Marlow, his gray hair sprawling in an untidy mass across his wide head, stood in the doorway. "Bring her right in, Van," he said.

Winston climbed down from his horse. He went to the wagon, waited for the driver to jump down. "You can give me a hand carrying Ella inside, Adams." Then he jerked his head at a couple of other men in his crew. "Keep an eye on Frazer. If he makes a break, you know what to do."

Two hill ranchers, Barton and Kerlan by name, shoved

183

a path along the walk and shouted at the Circle W owner. "What kind of a rigged-up deal are you pulling here, Winston."

An immediate air of tension slid along the crowd. Some men shifted position, trying to duck out of line. The Circle W punchers drew their guns and formed a protective circle about Frazer.

"There's nothing rigged up about this," snapped Winston. "We caught Frazer trying to run off with my wife. They were caught in a landslide. Ella's badly hurt."

"Maybe she wanted to run," said Barton.

Winston bridled. "You looking for trouble, Barton?"

Barton stood his ground. He was a lean-bodied man with sharp blue eyes and a slow, deliberate manner. "Not any. But Tom Frazer is a friend of mine. I don't figure him for a trick like that."

"Well, you figure wrong," growled Winston. "Ella's dying, and just as soon as Doc Marlow has a look at her I aim to see Frazer hung—and you can watch!"

"Do your talking later, Van!" said the doctor irritably. "Let's get Ella inside so I can see what can be done for her."

The doctor brushed aside several men and went to the bed of the wagon. Then, with Winston and Adams assisting him, he picked up Ella's limp form and gently carried her inside his office. A few of the curious followed them.

Frazer sat his horse in the midst of the Circle W crew. Sweat stood out on his cheeks from his surreptitious efforts to loosen the thin rope that locked his wrists together. He had been tugging and wrenching at them all during the long ride to town. The flesh around his wrists was raw and inflamed and pained him terribly. He had managed to spread his hands apart just a trifle. But it was not enough to get them free. And the thing that bothered him was that he knew he didn't have much time left.

Now he glanced at Barton and said, "Better stay out of it, Clem."

"Hell," said Barton, "what's a friend for? You weren't running off with Ella, were you?"

"No, Clem. I was on the way to the Pothook, heard the roar of the slide. When I got around that point of rock on the Dunbar road I found a smashed buckboard and Ella buried to her waist in rubble."

"Shut up!" snapped one of Frazer's guards. "We heard that story and it doesn't hold water."

Barton ignored the puncher and said to Frazer: "Was she alone?"

"Looked that way, Clem," said Frazer. "Didn't see anyone else around."

"That's enough for me," Barton told him. "This outfit isn't putting any rope around your neck if I can help it. I'll go see the sheriff."

"You're wasting your time," said one of the Circle W advance riders. "Landon's out of town."

At that moment Winston, Adams, and the rest of the curious who had piled into the doctor's office came shuffling out.

"What did the doc say?" one of Winston's punchers sang out.

"He can't tell until he's made a thorough examination," the rancher said. "He'll know how bad it is in a little while." Winston shouldered his way through the throng. Many of them were range drifters or punchers temporarily out of work. They had no particular sympathies, but the prospect of some excitement was enough to hold them here. "All right," Winston said. "Let's get on with the hanging."

"Not so fast!" yelled Barton. He had a gun in his hand and Kerlan had stepped a few paces to one side and also had drawn a Colt. "You're not hanging anybody tonight.

This looks like a frameup on Frazer to me. By God, there must be enough of Tom's friends in this crowd to put a stop to this damned nonsense." He whirled on the crowd. "Are you men going to let Winston's bunch run their own law on Frazer?"

"I reckon they are," said a new, threatening voice from the alley behind Barton. "Drop that gun and drop it fast, Barton!"

Barton made a half-turn, his face congealed in fury and surprise. Guy Thorpe sat in the shadows on a black horse. His gun was lined on Barton's back. He moved forward. Behind him trooped Pole Richmond, a bloody bandage around his head, and all of the Big T crew.

Barton had no choice. He dropped his Colt with a curse. Kerlan followed suit while the Big T riders pushed their way through the throng, taking up carefully selected positions.

Frazer watched this sudden turn of affairs and felt all hope die in him. With the sheriff out of town and most of his friends home with their own outfits he didn't have a chance. He looked at the crowd and saw a handful of familiar faces. But they were the faces of storekeepers, men who couldn't be expected to take any physical risks. Except for Barton and Kerlan there was no one he could count on. The few dirt farmers and hangers-on that made up the rest of the crowd would stay strictly neutral.

No, if he had any hope at all of being rescued it would be through the agency of Tex White. But he knew that Tex had hardly had enough time to round up the Roush and Simmons crowd and bring them on to town. Even an accusation tossed in the direction of Guy Thorpe would avail nothing in the face of this indifferent and callous mob. And Thorpe, wanting to protect his own hide, was playing Winston's game. Thorpe's bunch had tried once to kill him. Here was another chance!

Thorpe's hard drawl circulated through the tightly grouped men. "Me and the boys heard enough of what happened," he said, "to figure that there's only one play for Winston to make. Hell, you know what any one of you would do with anybody you caught stealing one of your cows or a horse! You'd shoot the jigger on sight and no questions asked. Well, a man that tries to put his hands on another man's wife rates even worse than a rustler in my book."

"But what kind of a book do you carry, Guy?" Frazer demanded. "And what's the color of it? Black?"

Fear churned muddily in Thorpe's eyes for a brief second. Then he said with a savage intensity, "We'll see how tough you talk with your neck stretching hemp, my friend!"

Once more Frazer debated telling the crowd that Thorpe was a rustler. But with only his word to back up the story it would mean nothing to any of the men except Barton and Kerlan—and their fangs had already been pulled. No, he needed Tex White and Roush and Simmons and others like them—men whose standing in the town meant something—to tell the story to. Then there would be action.

Desperately he wrenched at his bonds. The sharp cord dug into the bruised flesh of his wrists. It cut deeply, drawing blood. He gritted his teeth against the severe pain. If he could get free now he'd make a run for it through the crowd. Even surrounded as he was by the hostile Circle W crew and Thorpe's men on the outer flanks, they'd have a hard time hitting him once he piled off his horse and darted into the close-pressing throng.

Then the sound of a fast-moving horse drummed down the street. In the outflung light of a saloon Frazer saw that the rider was a girl. The next instant, as the girl drew

187

her mount to a rearing halt at the edge of the crowd, he saw that it was Margo.

"Tom!" she cried in sudden frenzy. Her eyes darted from Winston to Thorpe's sardonic, smiling face. She was bewildered. Some of the confusion got into her words. "What—what about the posse? I—I thought——"

Thorpe's eyes narrowed and his hard mouth flattened against his yellowed teeth. "Posse, hell!" he shouted. "Your ramrod's in a jam he won't get out of. Winston caught him running off with Ella." While the mob pressed close, sensing a new source of excitement, Thorpe added with wicked relish: "You're just in time to watch Frazer stretch a bit of hemp."

"You men are out of your minds!" Margo cried. Fear was like a weighted stone in her. But she showed Thorpe the edge of an anger that was pushing her toward recklessness. "Tom was with me at the Double-Y ranch just a little while ago."

"What does that prove, Margo?" Winston cut in. Then, before she could reply, he added: "How long ago was he there?"

"About an hour ago," the girl blurted. "He was riding to the Pothook to see Bassett about——"

"Margo!" Frazer's voice cut in quickly. "Stay out of this."

"But why, Tom?" Margo cried fiercely. "Why not let me tell them what happened——"

Thorpe, his face twisted in taut, straining lines, lifted his strident voice above Margo's. "We're wasting time talking here. It's obvious Margo is just trying to cover up for Frazer."

Margo raged at him. "You're afraid of what Tom knows."

"What's that, Margo?" demanded Barton from the

188

depths of the crowd. "Maybe it's something we'd all like to hear."

"Shut Barton up!" yelled Winston as he exchanged a sudden nervous glance with Thorpe.

There was a scuffle in the crowd. Barton cursed as a couple of Circle W hands moved in on him. He struggled briefly, then went down as a gun barrel slammed against the side of his head.

Margo pushed her horse forward, striving to get near to Frazer. "Tom," she said, "tell me what really happened."

"There's not much to tell," he said, facing her across a sea of sweat-grimed faces. "I started out for the Pothook. Riding along the Dunbar road I heard the roar of a landslide. When I got to that point of rock along the bluff I found a wrecked buckboard. Half-buried in the dirt and shale that had fallen from the cliff was Ella. Winston's bunch ran into me as I was about to get help for Ella."

Margo twisted in the saddle. She regarded Winston with a cold and studied antagonism. "And that's your basis for wanting to hang Tom?"

"She was running away," Winston snapped. "You'll find a smashed suitcase in that buckboard behind you. It was Ella's." Blood suffused his cheeks. His control began to slip. "I tell you Frazer's got a killing coming to him. He's always been sweet on Ella. Maybe you haven't had eyes to see that because you want Frazer for yourself."

An odd expression flickered in Margo's eyes. "You've got the wrong man," she said sharply. "I think I can tell you——"

Again Frazer's voice cut in to interrupt her. "Let it go, Margo."

She looked at him in perplexity. She saw the dull misery in his face. Suddenly she knew he was trying to protect the man they both realized was guilty. Her eyes darted a question at Frazer. His answer was a faint shrug of his broad shoulders.

"Come on, Van!" shouted Thorpe. "We've dallied long enough. Let's get this necktie party started."

"That's what I say!" shouted tall, lanky Pole Richmond as he cut a lane through the ranks of the crowd to reach Van Winston's side. His evil grinning face jutted toward Frazer. "Here's your finish, bucko. I'm going to enjoy watching you choke."

Though Frazer's features were haggard and twisted with strain, his eyes showed a smokier color. They were narrowed and intent. While he struggled with the pigging string on his wrists he said in a voice sharp as a sword, "I'm not dead yet, Pole. You tried to kill me once. Remember?"

Margo whipped up her horse. The animal's powerful shoulders struck two men blocking her path. They jumped out of the way, mumbling and complaining. She raked the crowd with a scornful challenge.

"Aren't there any men among you with the sense and the courage to stop this ugly farce?" She glanced from one to the other. She picked out a few of the store-keepers. "Johnson! Begley! Farning! What are you doing here? How can you permit this to go on? Get out your guns!"

For a moment there was no answer. Then Johnson's meek voice replied. "This is none of our business, Margo. We're family men. We don't aim to invite any trouble."

A hard laugh spilled from Thorpe. It was taken up by his callous crew. It spread to Winston's armed bunch.

Margo's angry cry tore at the crowd. "And you call yourselves men! You're worse than coyotes!" With a savage gesture her hand sped to the .38 revolver at her hip. She flipped it into her hand. She drove her plunging mare right at Guy Thorpe, firing as she charged.

190

At the instant Margo's .38 roared one of the Big T riders crowded against her and slapped at her arm. The bullet meant for Thorpe drilled the air above his head.

In the resulting confusion Frazer yelled: "Margo, stay out of this!"

Then Winston cried, "Thorpe, get her out of here!"

Thorpe and the man who had spoiled Margo's aim wrestled with the furiously angry girl. Thoroughly outraged now, Margo tried to train the gun on Thorpe again. But the weapon was wrested from her fingers. Then strong arms hauled her out of the saddle and dragged her to the ground. She kept crying, "Tom! Tom!" as she fought the men who were dragging her away from the middle of the street.

Frazer dug his heels into the flanks of his horse in a wild frenzy to reach Margo. But the press of horses around him was too great. Winston closed in on one side. A knuckled fist swished through the air and caught him on the side of the jaw. Then Pole Richmond jammed his big gelding forward. He had a rope in his hand, a noose already fashioned.

"Here we go, Van!" he said. "We'll use my rope!"

19   The noises pulsing through Bill Corey's skull rolled in from vast distances. They swelled and retreated like the rhythmic beat of surf. He seemed to be in a deep black well. Now and then there were weird flashes of light. But always the darkness swept in again. It was a thick, miasmic fog. He imagined he was swimming in a gritty, sandy sea. His arms moved convulsively. But something had snared his legs. They were mired in slick, slimy mud. No matter how he thrashed about he could not free his lower limbs.

The noises came on again. They were louder now. At first it was just an odd jumble of sound. Then as he floated in that dark sea of semi-consciousness he sorted the sounds into voices. But they weren't clear. The edges of the words were ragged and split. Suddenly the voices were cut off. He heard a creak and rattle, another sound like the drum of hoofs. The smell of dust reached him.

At last he opened his eyes. That hoof clatter was distinct now, but going away. He found himself on his back. There was a fierce ache in his side. His head throbbed dully. He tried to orient himself.

The sky was above him, the white flash of stars seemingly very near. Moonlight bathed the shaly slope before him. It rose in a steep slant—that slope. Then, abruptly,

192

memory returned to him. And with memory came horror and fear.

He recalled the wild ride in the buckboard with Ella, the sudden roar of sound that was followed by the suffocating rush of the landslide. The wagon had been wrecked. He remembered whipping up the team in a frantic effort to gallop clear of the slide. But he'd been too late. He and Ella had caught the full brunt of that mountainous fall of loose earth.

He saw that he was in the culvert beside the road and half-concealed behind thick brush. Loose shale and dirt covered his legs. That accounted for the nightmare of mud he had dreamed about. Somehow he had been thrown clear when the wagon heeled over.

But what about Ella?

That question spitted his nerves on sharp spikes. He dreaded the search that lay ahead of him. It required a great effort of his will to scramble clear of the confining shale. Once free, he climbed out of the culvert. The exertion started his wound to bleeding again. Hot needles drilled through the lacerated flesh.

He reached the road and for the first time had a clear look at the havoc created by the avalanche. All around him, as though tossed by a giant hand, were huge chunks of rock torn from the bluff. Among the rocks and piled in three- and four-foot depths rose a mound of dirt and scattered strips of shale.

The wagon was a total wreck. It had overturned. One smashed wheel stuck out of the earth. Splintered boards from the bed of the vehicle were strewn about. One horse, deeply trapped in the rubble, was dead. The other animal had somehow gotten free of the wreckage and was now grazing at the edge of the trees.

Corey slithered through the shale. He made a complete circuit of the landslide. At intervals he dropped to his knees and pawed through the dirt. Nowhere did he see any sign of Ella. His fear grew by leaps and bounds. It occurred to him that she might be buried at the bottom of the rubble. If that were so, he could do nothing to help her. It would take a big crew of men, armed with shovels and spades, to clear the road and probe to the bottom of the avalanche.

No, he told himself, Ella must have been thrown clear just as he had been. It had to be that way. Yet a thorough search of the culvert revealed nothing. It was then that Corey pinned all his hopes on the horsemen he'd heard in the vicinity when he was regaining consciousness. Perhaps they had found Ella and taken her into town. In any event, he decided that he'd have to run the risk of going to Two Forks to find out. He'd never rest until he knew how Ella was.

Though he was aware of the danger involved he no longer cared. If any of the Big T riders were in town he could count on trouble. They wouldn't take Pole Richmond's killing lying down. They'd be after his hide.

But nothing mattered now. He'd burned all his bridges. He'd broken with Thorpe. It was too late to change that. He'd killed Richmond and he'd tried to run off with another man's wife. He'd gone all the way. He was through in Two Forks. It was over the hill for him. And he'd have to take the trail alone. Whether Ella was alive or dead, he couldn't do anything in that direction. The landslide had seen to that.

It was time to ride out. But first he had to satisfy himself about Ella. That much had to be done even though his strength was at a low ebb.

Scrambling through the rubble to the idly grazing horse, he took the gelding by the bridle and pulled him toward the slide. Using a mound of dirt as a platform, Corey succeeded in climbing onto the horse's back. However, the first step the gelding took told Corey he was in for an ordeal of physical punishment. His side throbbed intolerably. Weakness was a flood tide overwhelming all his senses. But he set his will against the pain and the weakness and pushed on.

Corey lost all sense of time after that. The steady jog of the horse, the heavy sledging rhythm of agony in his body merged into one endless nightmare. Several times he nearly slipped from the bare back of the horse. Each time a frantic clutch at the animal's thick mane saved him from a fall. He knew if he ever toppled off the horse he wouldn't be able to muster the strength to remount.

After what seemed an age he saw the yellow shine of lights. There was a cluster of them. They cut a wide swathe in the blackness of the night. He knew, then, that he was on the outskirts of Two Forks.

He rode down a short slope, saw the head of the main street before him, and quickly steered the horse into the rear alley. Perspiration covered him from head to foot, yet there was a deep-seated chill in his bones. He understood the significance of that. His fever was mounting.

He knew he needed a doctor, and wondered if he could risk going to Doc Marlow. Immediately he told himself this was impossible—especially if Ella had been brought in. There would be a crowd of people around plus Winston's bunch. No, Marlow was out. If he were going to see a doctor he'd have to wait until he got to Dunbar—if he ever got there.

The horse threaded its way through the assorted litter of the alley. Tin cans and crates and boxes covered the ground in back of the stores. He was halfway down the first street when he heard the clamor of voices. Shouts and yells filled the air. Gritting his teeth against the pain that assailed him, Corey pushed on at a faster gait.

He crossed an empty side street, moved along the rear

lots behind the main street. The racket grew louder. Someone shouted Tom Frazer's name. Corey stopped. His heart suddenly pumped a hot surge of blood into his head. The voice that had cried his name sounded oddly like Margo's.

The feeling of trouble hummed through Corey. He slid from the back of the horse at the junction of another narrow alley which led to the main street. He went forward a few steps before his legs gave way and he fell. Again he felt his heart pumping inside his chest. His hand scraped against his side. It came away wet. That was his blood, steadily seeping from the bullet gash below his ribs.

Corey shook his head. His vision was hazy. Cobwebs were strung across his brain. There was a dry ache in his throat. He got his hands underneath his body and pushed upward. Somehow he scrambled erect.

Supporting himself against the frame wall of the hotel, he stumbled toward the street. A cluster of men was gathered in front of the hotel. Others milled about in the center of the street. Some of the men were on horseback. A wild confusion of voices filled the night.

Corey reached the edge of the shadows along the boardwalk. Somewhere near by he heard a couple of men talking. Ella's name was mentioned. He caught the words "Doc Marlow" and "she's badly hurt" and felt a brief measure of relief in knowing that Ella had been rescued from the slide.

Then he stiffened with shock when he saw Margo seated on her horse, her face flushed with anger, as she exchanged angry words with Thorpe. He heard the Big T owner tell Margo that Tom Frazer had tried to run off with Ella and that the crowd intended to hang him for it.

Those last words jerked Corey's head up. From his crouched position in the darkness of the alley he finally saw Frazer. Two of the riders who had been shielding him from view shifted their mounts. Corey was startled to see that Frazer was a prisoner. His hands were bound behind his back and there was a grim, badgered look about him.

Corey's teeth grated together. This was altogether worse than he had anticipated. Not only had his and Ella's plan to escape blown up in their faces, but by some wicked quirk of fate Frazer—the man he had wronged in so many ways—had walked into the situation and was being accused of something he—Corey—had done.

A bitter sensation of self-abasement slogged through Corey. He had made a mess of his own life. He had robbed and cheated. He had betrayed the only real friend he'd ever owned. Now that friend was about to die because of him.

Sweat oozed out of his forehead. He forgot the knives of pain that lashed at his side. He forgot the terrible weakness that chained his muscles. He had room for just one thing in his mind. He had to get Frazer out of this jam.

While he lingered in the gloom he heard the argument between Margo and Thorpe continue. Then Barton's strident yell cut across the sibilant murmur of the crowd. Van Winston's curt order to his men produced the brief scuffle across the street that saw Barton struck down.

Corey drew out his gun. His arm shook when he leveled it. Three men came along the walk. He retreated, thinking they planned to enter the alley. But they pushed closer to the fringes of the mob. Margo was talking again. Corey listened intently when she cried that Frazer was the wrong man. Then he received his second shock when the knot of riders around Frazer parted once more and Pole Richmond, a dirty bandage fastened around his forehead, appeared. Corey was amazed to see the Big T ramrod. His last memory of Richmond was of seeing him fall forward under his smoking gun while a red weal of blood trickled down his forehead.

Watching Richmond, Corey felt hot anger come to a quick boil in him. His fingers tightened around the handle of his Colt. At this precise moment his attention was pulled away from Richmond by a shout from Guy Thorpe, urging Winston to get the hanging started.

Corey almost charged straight into the crowd. But as he took the first tentative forward step Margo sent her horse crashing into the men who blocked her way. Corey heard her berate the mob. He heard her call upon them to stop the hanging.

A sudden idea leaped into Corey's brain. He didn't think Margo would be able to provoke the crowd into action. It was, for the most part, a strictly partisan group. The others—the nesters and townsmen—would stay neutral. He could expect no help from any of them.

But there was one thin chance of breaking up this grim gathering. Even at that, a lot would depend on luck.

Retreating along the alley, Corey moved around to the untended rear door of the hotel. He crept into the darkened hallway. The lobby, as he expected, was deserted. He hurried to the stairs. With one hand clutching his torn side and the other gripping his .45, he climbed to the second floor and swung down the corridor that led to the front of the building.

20   Frazer tugged desperately at the tight cords that bound his wrists. He felt them give a trifle more. But was it enough to get his hands free?

A rider behind him yelled a warning to Pole Richmond. "Watch out, Pole. Frazer's trying to get his hands loose."

"Let him!" scoffed Richmond, pushing his horse close to Frazer. "In a minute or two he'll be dragging his weight at the end of this rope!"

Noose in hand, the Big T foreman leaned toward Frazer, ready to flip the ugly circle of rope around Frazer's throat.

"Drop that rope or I'll put a bullet through your heart!"

The order was a harsh, strident cry slicing like a bowie knife through the taut stillness that had suddenly fallen upon the mob of men gathered in the middle of Two Forks' main street.

Frazer's heart skipped a beat as he recognized Bill Corey's voice. He looked toward the slanting board roof that covered the plank walk in front of the hotel. Every man in the crowd followed his gaze.

Standing in full view of the throng was Corey. He was a rumpled, disheveled figure. His clothes looked as if he had slept in them for a week. His hair hung down across his face. He swayed a little as if he were drunk. But the six-gun in his right hand was as steady as a rock. And there was no mistaking the deadly set of his thin mouth.

"Corey, stay out of this!" yelled Van Winston.

"Like hell I will!" snapped Corey. The gun barrel in his fist dipped up and down in a menacing gesture. "Make one move for your cutter, Richmond, and you're a dead man." Corey's mouth flattened against his teeth in a wicked snarl. "This time," he added viciously, "I'll do more than crease your skull."

"Get out of here before it's too late," warned Winston.

"Shut up and listen to me, Winston," grated Corey. His vision blurred for a moment. He swayed, then caught himself. "You're looking for the hombre that ran away with your wife tonight. Well, I'm your huckleberry!"

There was a gasp from the crowd, followed by a low, aroused murmuring. Corey saw the massed hostility of the Big T crew. They were primed to go into action against him. Thorpe had his gun fisted. It was lifting slowly, swinging around toward him. He knew he didn't have much time. He glanced swiftly at Frazer, wondering how much of a chance for freedom he was really giving his friend. Frazer was pretty well hemmed in on all sides. And with his hands roped behind his back he'd be hard put to maneuver his horse.

Pole Richmond still held the noose in his hand. Frazer watched him intently. The ramrod had backed his horse a pace or two away. The crowd was like a lit fuse, sputtering away. He saw Thorpe sneaking his Colt around. He'd have to shout a warning to Corey.

"I've got the man I want!" roared Winston. "Put your gun away."

"No, damn you, Winston!" shouted Corey. "And here's something else for the whole blasted town to chew on. It's time Two Forks found out about the kind of dirty game you and——"

Corey never got a chance to finish. Frazer saw Thorpe's gun arm whip around in a rapid arc. He yelled, "Bill, watch Thorpe!" Then muzzle light jumped from the Big T owner's gun bore.

Pain and shock dug deep furrows in Corey's drawn cheeks. He folded up, dropped to his knees. From that position he hauled his Colt up and fired at Thorpe. An insane laugh bubbled from Corey's mouth. Then he sagged down on his face. He didn't even see that Thorpe's plunging horse had carried the Big T owner out of the path of his shot. The bullet intended for Thorpe struck one of his riders and sent the man hurtling to the ground.

At the flash of Thorpe's gun Frazer gave a final frenzied wrench at his bonds. The pigging string loosened. Suddenly his hands were free. He sank his spurs into the gelding's flanks. The animal squealed and jumped full tilt into the two Circle W riders blocking his path. One man was jarred out of the saddle as the gelding struck his horse with pile-driving force. The other man levered his gun. A red streamer of flame slid past Frazer's right cheek. Then he smashed the fellow's jaw with a looping right. The man fell away.

Frazer charged toward the walk. Guns boomed behind him. The gelding hit a running man. A frightened scream rent the air. The man went down, rolling away from the gelding's hoofs.

At the edge of the walk Frazer leaped from the saddle. A deadly destructiveness propelled him now. He kept seeing Corey go down under the fire from Thorpe's gun. His throat still crawled with the imagined feel of the noose. And he knew that tonight would settle many things. But whatever was ahead of him, he was free and he had his own two hands to battle with. That was all he ever asked.

A Big T rider cut along the hitch rack toward him. The man's gun bloomed ruddily in the night. A porch post took the full brunt of the slug as Frazer dived under the rail and made for the hotel veranda. A short, bowlegged man on foot moved toward him. Frazer wasn't sure of the fellow's intentions. He hit him with the heel of his hand, straight-arming him on the jaw and knocking him full away.

"After him, you buckos!" shouted Winston.

"Bottle him up in the hotel!" Richmond yelled.

Frazer plunged through the open doorway. A volley of shots followed him. One slug splintered the lintel of the door. A second bullet tugged at his shirt sleeve. The tumult rose behind him. Boots thumped the walk. The wail of six-guns rose in an angry dirge.

He gained the stairway, flung himself up the steps, two at a time, though the effort tore at his lungs. A wild-flung bullet from a Circle W puncher slapped at the darkness of the upper story. Frazer whirled toward the front of the hotel. He struck a door at the end of the corridor, flung it open with a sweep of his arm.

Once inside he slammed it shut, flipped the bolt into its slot. He was breathing hard now. Time was running out. He heard the racket on the stairs that told him his pursuers were close behind.

He was fully aware that by running into the hotel he had stepped into a trap. But there was Corey to think of. He couldn't let Corey lie there on the porch roof. He had to see what could be done for Corey before he made his own break.

The window of the darkened room made a pale wedge of light in the gloom. Frazer stumbled to it. He found it already open. He bent his long body, scrambled out onto

202

the tilted roof. Behind him he heard the smashed weight of several bodies hitting the bolted door. Then came the booming roar of several guns.

"Try the other doors!" somebody yelled.

There was a rush for one of the other doors. Again came the splintering crash of several huge men flinging themselves against resisting wooden panels.

Frazer's sun-browned jaw knotted. If those doors only held out for a few minutes.

He slid down the roof. Corey was lying in a limp heap before him. A crowd of men still surged in the street. Almost flat on his belly, he crawled down to Corey. He didn't know if anyone in the crowd had seen him. But it was a chance he had to take. However, from the clamor in the hall beyond him he gathered that most of Winston's and Thorpe's men must have charged into the hotel.

Frazer tugged at Corey. "Bill! Can you talk? It's me—Tom!"

Corey stirred, rolled half on his side. A bloody bubble broke from his lips. Frazer felt suddenly sick and desperate. Corey's breathing was a thin, agonized thread of sound. A shudder racked his body.

"I—I'm going out, Tom," Corey whispered.

"I'll get Thorpe," grated Frazer. He heard the solid smash of bodies hitting the door of the room he had gone through. In a second or two Winston's men would gain admittance. Still he waited. "Damn it, Bill. Why did you do it? I—I mean Ella."

"I—I've been a fool—all my life," gasped Corey. His lips twisted in a grin. But it was a painful effort. "Should have listened to you, kid. We—we might have gone places together." Corey's voice dropped. A faint rattle sounded in his throat. His lips writhed with bright red blood. "Get Thorpe—for—me. Thorpe—and—Winston are handling the—the rustling together."

Frazer felt a dull ache of sorrow inside him. Corey was dying. There was nothing he could do for him. He put his face close to Corey's. "Bill," he said, "are you sure about that?"

There was more shouting from inside the hotel. Someone fired a brace of bullets. In that great racket Frazer barely caught Corey's labored reply.

"Yeah. I—I ought—to—be sure. I—I've been riding with them."

The shock of that announcement was like a dash of cold water in Frazer's face. "Bill," he said, "you're out of your head."

Corey's eyes were blurred and weary. His shaggy head moved slightly in negation. "Wish I—I was," he murmured. His voice was fading fast. The cords of his throat stood out, quivering, with the intense strain of bringing out his words. "Sorry—Tom. I—I'm one hell of a friend." His right hand groped along his body. It lifted toward Frazer. There was a Colt in it. "My—my gun," Corey gasped. "You—you may need it. Get away while——"

The voice died away as if something had blocked Corey's throat. He stiffened in Frazer's arms, then fell back limp in death.

A hot stab of agony raked Frazer's vitals. He blinked his eyes. His teeth ground together in a silent oath.

A splintering crash, followed by a wild, triumphant yell from the hotel corridor, brought Frazer to his feet. The weathered frame structure trembled to the heavy tramp of booted feet in the room beyond. One of the Circle W punchers appeared in the window. He fired at Frazer's crouching shape. The bullet sped wide. Frazer whirled, Corey's gun in his fist, and drove the man from the window with one telling shot.

Somewhere inside the hotel another crash sounded.

Frazer left Corey, ran along the sloping porch roof. He pumped a slug into the adjoining window as a man's thick figure outlined the pane. The glass blew inward and the man spun away, screaming.

A half-dozen horses were tied to the hitching rail at the far corner of the hotel. Frazer stumbled across the uneven sloping roof. He went down on one knee as a new attack from one of the windows sent several bullets singing over his head. He swiveled around, snapped a shot through each window. Then he rose, lurched to the roof edge.

Directly below him three chaps-clad men on foot ran along the plank sidewalk to cut him off. A red flame streak gushed from a tilted gun barrel aimed in Frazer's direction. He jumped right into their midst. His left boot struck one man on the neck below the ear and felled him. Then the other two punchers went down with Frazer in a threshing tangle of arms and legs.

A wildly flailing fist grazed Frazer's jaw. He shoved the weight of one fellow's body from him. Propped on one knee he pistol-whipped the remaining man on the right temple and rolled free. He got up. There was a tumult of noise all around him. Men were running toward him from all directions. Guns were booming from the hotel windows. But he ducked under the hitch rack. He freed the reins of a bony gray gelding and lifted himself into the saddle. Rearing away from the tie rail, he sent the horse pounding down the street. At the first intersection he swung east, cutting through a dark alley at a fast gallop.

After a hundred yards he struck some brush. The gouge of Frazer's spurs sent the half-frightened horse right through the bushes. Once in that frail cover he turned south again, riding hard and gradually angling back toward the main road.

He knew it would not take long for pursuit to shape up. Neither Winston nor Thorpe could afford to let him run free now. But with a strong horse under him Frazer wasn't worried. The only thing that did bother him was the failure of Tex White to put in an appearance with the riders from Dale Roush's and Ad Simmons's outfits. He had been counting on those two ranches for help. Whatever the cause of delay, it was now his only logical course of retreat.

Five minutes of steady, fast traveling brought him back to the wagon road that ran from Two Forks past Roush's eastern grazing lands and on to Dragoon over the mountains to the south.

Frazer didn't slacken his pace when he reached the road. He kept on at a dead run until the sound of a big party of riders sent its unmistakable vibrations through the night. Frazer hauled in the gray. He slid from the saddle. Paused at the edge of the road, he decided that the racket was approaching out of the south. With luck it would be Tex White and the bunch from the Roush and Simmons spreads.

He got back on the gray, jammed fresh bullets into the fired chambers of Corey's six-gun, and rode slowly forward.

In a few moments a column of horsemen topped a little rise several hundred yards away and clattered toward him. Gun in hand, Frazer continued on at a slow trot. The leaders spotted him at once. The column spread out across the road and a long yell challenged him.

"Who's that?"

It was Tex White, and Frazer immediately answered. "Frazer—here!"

Another yell, this one more pronounced, rolled up echoes in the night. The riders whipped toward him in a boiling cloud of dust. As they pulled up in the middle of the road Frazer had a quick glimpse of Dale Roush and Ad Simmons flanking Tex White. Then a little behind those three he saw the still more welcome figure of Sheriff Fred Landon.

"Something go wrong in town, Tom?" Tex White asked.

"Plenty," said Frazer. "But I'm glad you're all here. We're going to need every man's gun."

The sheriff pushed his horse forward. "What's up, Tom?"

"Hell's busted loose for sure."

"Tex told us about the stolen beef in the hills," said Landon. "I'd just ridden into Roush's place from Dragoon. If you can lead us to those cow critters we'll lay a trap for those Big T waddies."

"No time for that now," said Frazer, talking fast while he cocked his head to listen for sounds of horsemen coming from town. "The Big T and the Circle W are both on my tail and spoiling for a fight." Then in a few concise words he told all that had happened since he first ran across the smashed buckboard on the Dunbar road.

"You say Ella's hurt and Corey's dead?" exclaimed Landon.

"Yeah." Frazer's voice was dull and leaden. "Doc Marlow's taking care of Ella now. Don't know if she'll pull through. But Thorpe got Bill right after Bill tried to tell the crowd that Winston and Thorpe were handling the rustling together."

"God, I can hardly believe that!" muttered Roush, a heavily built man with ruddy full cheeks and dark blue eyes.

"But don't forget that Corey owned up to riding with the Big T bunch," pointed out Landon. "A fellow that's dying can be pretty well figured to tell the truth."

"I hear riders coming!" called Tex White. "Sounds like a big party too!"

"That'll be Winston and Thorpe," murmured Frazer.

Landon took immediate charge. "I'll handle this," he said. "No shooting unless they fire first."

"All right," said Frazer. "But spread out and be ready to burn some powder."

"I'm ready," growled Roush. "If Thorpe and Winston are the buckos who've been running off my beef along with everybody else's I sure as hell want to get in on this ruckus."

The racket of the approaching party of horsemen mounted to a heavy din. Then around a bend in the road the riders came on. Suddenly seeing the spread-out bunch of men blocking their advance they pulled to a halt. Moonlight glittered on rifles and six-guns.

"Winston, is that you?" called Landon.

"Yeah, Landon." Winston's voice was a guttural growl. "We're after Tom Frazer."

"I'm right here, Van," said Frazer, and added on a shrill note, "And the sheriff's heard my story."

Roush's angry voice cut in, "You and Thorpe have done your last rustling in Two Forks."

"Shut up, Roush!" shouted Landon. "I'm handling this." The sheriff raised his voice. "Winston, you and your party will turn around and head back to town. We'll——"

The roar of a gunshot, punctuated by a crimson spear of flame, broke into the lawman's words. He uttered a strangled gasp and pitched forward against his saddle horn.

Frazer spurred up to him. "Landon——!"

The sheriff lifted a pain-racked face. "I—I'm all right. Gun them down. We—we've got our answer!"

That brief exchange between Frazer and the sheriff had taken just a few seconds. But suddenly the crashing beat of guns tore the night into shreds. Landon got a hold on

208

himself. He straightened with an effort, curveted his horse to one side.

"Spread out! Spread out!" Frazer warned the riders at his back as Winston and Thorpe led their men in a swift, savage onslaught upon the posse.

21   That first wild rush saw two of Roush's punchers go down. Frazer held his ground for a moment, lining his sights on a rider's heaving shape charging toward him. He felt the hot whisper of lead pass him by. Then he saw a riderless horse bolt across the posse line at a severe tangent and knew he'd scored a hit.

Dust swirled about the road in a heavy cloud. Horses whinnied, men yelled and shouted to one another. The darkness was alive to the winking red glare of six-guns. The acrid taint of powder smoke hung in the still air. Frazer saw with abrupt concern that the brunt of Winston's attack was hitting the center of the posse's line. He swung his gelding around, started a retreat.

"Drop back and fan around them!" he called out.

Roush and Simmons cut in beside him, shooting as they came.

"We've got to suck them into our center, then outflank them," Frazer told them.

"Good idea!" panted Roush. "I'll take the left flank."

He spurred his horse away, singing out to a half-dozen of his men to follow him. Frazer and Simmons immediately dropped farther back. Bullets swept over them in a lethal spray. A wedge of riders angled toward them. Frazer ducked into the trees, Simmons on his heels.

"This way!" shouted Frazer.

A few yards off the road he knifed in and out of the brush. The clatter of shooting remained undiminished. Suddenly he cut sharply back to the road again. A knot of four riders were spurring south.

"Come and get it, friends!" Frazer cried.

He waited a fraction of a second. All four riders twisted in the saddle, alert to the attack on this new quarter. Their guns swung around in a glittering arc. Two of them never got to fire their pieces. Frazer dropped one man with a snap shot from the hip. Roush unseated the other with a bullet high in the shoulder.

Panic hit the remaining two punchers. They yelled: "Big T! Here!"

Frazer rode in among them. His down-chopping gun caught one fellow on the head and spilled him from the saddle. The fourth man bolted into the brush beside the road. Frazer took after him. But at the edge of the trees he skidded to a halt and turned to face a wave of Big T and Circle W riders galloping back toward town. Caught in the pocket created by Frazer's flanking maneuver, they were making a desperate dash through the gantlet of lead hurled by the posse.

Frazer spotted Guy Thorpe at the head of the phalanx. The Big T owner was lashing his horse to a full gallop, intent only upon escaping the trap. Frazer cut toward him and yelled: "Thorpe!"

The renegade rancher recognized Frazer. He swept out his gun and fired across the saddle. The shot was a clear miss. Frazer fired at Thorpe's bobbing shape and saw Thorpe's tall figure jerk under the solid thump of lead. Thorpe's horse carried him for fifty feet before he fell to the side.

Roush and Simmons were yelling somewhere near by. From both sides of the road came a raking volley that took its toll of the Circle W and Big T riders. Three more

211

saddles were emptied. Frazer cut alongside the fleeing renegades. A gun blazed close to his face, the slug narrowly missing his cheek.

He looked up, saw the hate-filled countenance of Pole Richmond. The white bandage circling the Big T ramrod's forehead was a sure target in the uncertain light.

"Now we'll end it, Pole!" Frazer said, prodding his gelding into a faster run.

Richmond, sensing his own finish, pumped another shot at Frazer. It burned across the flesh of Frazer's upper left arm. Frazer lifted his own Colt, flipped the hammer. He felt the kick of the weapon's recoil against his wrist. Richmond's gurgling cry of pain was almost lost in the thunder of hoofs. The Big T ramrod half-lifted out of his saddle, then pitched headfirst to the road.

Simultaneously a riderless mount crashed into Frazer's gelding. Both horses went down. Frazer barely freed his boots from the oxbows in time to escape being crushed under the rolling weight of his horse. He hit the ground with a solid jolt, scrambled clear.

The gelding was up almost instantly, unhurt by the collision. Frazer hobbled over to the animal, grabbed the bridle, and swung aboard. Sheriff Landon's deep call reached him from the rear. He saw the last of the Circle W and Big T riders go past him in a blur of speed.

Frazer cut back into the middle of the road. Other riders converged upon him from the trees and brush. Landon, holding himself stiffly in the saddle, came up with a few others.

"You going to let the rest of them get away?" Frazer demanded.

"Hell, no!" said Landon. He had his left hand pressed to his side. His shirt, in the region of his lower ribs, was wet with blood. "You fellows will have to carry on without me. But I want those men caught or run clear out of

212

the country. Winston and Thorpe gave themselves away when they fired on us tonight."

"Let's go," said Roush. "They'll head straight for the hills—maybe stop off at the Big T and the Circle W for their bedrolls if they have time."

Frazer started off with them. Landon called him back.

"Tom, you stick with me. You've done enough. I'll want you to help round up some other men to see about those stolen cattle." The sheriff nodded to Dale Roush. "Go ahead, Roush. Take them away!"

With a yell Roush led the posse away down the road at a fast run. In a moment they vanished around a bend though the echoes of their hard travel lingered for some time.

"How many men did we lose?" Frazer asked somberly.

"Four or five," said the sheriff. "But only one fellow is dead—a puncher from Roush's outfit. The others will pull through, I reckon." Landon peered closely at Frazer. "You see any sign of Winston?"

"He got away. At that he was luckier than Richmond and Thorpe."

"They were downed?" Landon asked.

"Yeah. Richmond is through. I'm sure of that." He told the sheriff of their final encounter. "About Thorpe I'm not sure. I drilled him, saw him fall, but that's all."

"We'll have a look," suggested Landon, "then head for town and get a couple of buckboards out here to bring the wounded in."

The two men skirted the edge of the road, watching carefully for fallen men. They came upon two wounded Roush punchers before finding Guy Thorpe. The Big T owner had been shot high in the chest and seemed to be in bad shape. But he was still breathing.

"I'd like to get Thorpe into Two Forks for Doc Marlow to fix up," said Landon. "Hurt the way he is, he

213

might do some talking that'll give us an open-and-shut case against Winston."

"After what happened you won't need it," said Frazer. "Firing on your bunch marked him good."

"Right. But a little extra evidence like a confession from Thorpe will wind everything up in a legal fashion."

They were almost within sight of Two Forks before the sheriff spoke again.

"Do you figure Winston will run?" he asked. "Don't forget there's Ella to think about."

"I've been wondering about that," said Frazer, pausing to reload his Colt from his shell belt. He thrust the weapon back into the leather holster. "It depends on which he values more—Ella or his own hide. She's a sick girl and may not be able to be moved for days. He's through in Two Forks. He knows that. I doubt if he'll risk his neck and come back for her."

"I reckon you're right," acknowledged the lawman. His face was gray and stained with sweat.

Frazer noted his distress. "Can you make it, Fred?"

"Yeah," said Landon. "Not far now."

They topped a slight knoll. Below them the lights of the town made an oblong yellow wedge of brilliance in the steel-black night.

They struck the first intersection and pushed on toward the next street. Lights from the hotel a hundred yards farther on winked across the road's gray dust. The sound of their travel drew a knot of men from one of the saloons. A few others hurried to the plank walks from the hotel veranda.

"It's the sheriff!" someone yelled. "And Frazer's with him!"

Frazer's hand crept to his gun. He wasn't sure of the temper of these men. True, the real troublemakers in the lynch mob had been the Big T and Circle W punchers.

214

But he wasn't taking any chances of being knocked out of the saddle by some gun-crazy fool.

The sheriff pushed out ahead of Frazer. His voice sounded a warning to the crowd. "Hold everything, gents! Tom Frazer's in the clear. The Big T and Circle W are the outfits I'm after tonight!"

A surprised murmur rippled through the fast-growing knot of men gathered in front of the hotel. There was a sudden flash of light from Doc Marlow's house as the door opened and closed. Margo came through and pushed out into the street. She saw Tom, called his name, and ran forward.

Frazer lifted his hand to her in greeting. Then his eyes caught a flicker of movement in the shadows of an alley he was passing. His keyed-up nerves telegraphed a warning to his brain. He was twisting in the saddle and driving the gelding toward the plank sidewalk when a ruddy lance of flame leaped out of the alley toward him. There was the immediately following roar of a shot.

The gelding staggered in mid-stride. The ambush slug meant for Frazer hit the horse's shoulder. Frazer felt the horse going down and jumped clear. He landed on hands and knees in the dust, hearing Margo's frightened cry and an aroused shout from the waiting crowd.

The ambusher fired one more wild shot. Dust spouted into Frazer's eyes as the bullet fell short. He lifted his gun, pumped a slug toward the spot where he had seen the ambusher's muzzle flare. But the pounding beat of feet running down the alley told him that the fellow was in full flight.

"Frazer!" the sheriff yelled. "Wait!"

But Frazer was in no mood to wait for anyone. This was his fight and his fight alone. He knew who the ambusher was. It had to be Van Winston. Pole Richmond was dead. Guy Thorpe was badly wounded out on the

Dragoon road. As for the remainder of the Circle W and Big T crews, they were men who would be looking after their own skins now that their respective outfits were finished. Theirs was a shallow loyalty bought with gun-slick wages and easily cast aside.

The only man with a stake in the game was Van Winston. For years he'd been the big augur on the range. But he'd been greedy for more land, more cattle, more power. Tonight's fight on the Dragoon road and the definite linking of his outfit with the rustling had shown Winston clearly enough that his reign as kingpin of Two Forks had terminated.

He was a man with nothing to fight for. He had a wife who obviously didn't want him and had tried to run away with another man. There was nothing for Winston to do but run.

Yet, knowing the temper of the man, the stubborn and inexorable drive of his will, Frazer saw that it was inevitable for Winston to stay on long enough to strike a telling blow at the man who symbolized his own ruin. And that man, Frazer realized, was himself.

Two Forks was now too big for the two of them. Winston would stay to kill him or be killed. That much was sure. Winston could be a bulldog with a bulldog's tenacity when he wanted something bad enough. And right now he wanted Frazer dead.

But he was pitting himself against a man even more tenacious and dangerous than himself. For Frazer's life had been a succession of hard risks. Action and violence were the wine of his existence. There was nothing he relished more than a fight. And with the memory of Bill Corey's death to goad him on, he was recklessly agreeable to settling with Winston.

A cold, destructive fury sent him up from the dust of the street in a headlong charge toward the alley. He tucked under a hitching rail, pounded across a section of plank sidewalk, and entered the narrow areaway between the Mercantile and a feed store.

Far down the alley a gun roared and a bullet whined along the frame side of the feed store. As he lifted his Colt to return the shot he saw the heavy, running shape of Winston vanish around the rear of the building.

Grimly Frazer plunged on. He was aware of the risk he ran. Winston might be hiding just beyond the rear wall of the feed store, waiting to swing around and blast him at close range. But Frazer was too wild, too impetuous to permit any such consideration to halt his rush. He had his gun at full cock, ready to trade shots with the rancher at a second's notice.

Somewhere behind him he heard the yelling of the crowd. Once he imagined he heard Margo's high-pitched voice calling him. Then he reached the end of the alley, took a headlong plunge past it, whirling to face the rear lots and half-expecting to be greeted by the roar of a six-gun.

But the darkened area behind the feed store was empty. Winston had fled to some other point of vantage. Frazer stopped, flattened against the wall, and listened for the sound of a running horse. All he heard was the hubbub in the street.

Breathing hard from his sprint down the alley, Frazer slid along the wall of the feed store. The next building jutted out more and he had to circle several old barrels and crates. He covered half a block in that fashion. All his nerves were strung out tight and fine. His eyes were narrow, his face drawn and thoroughly hard.

He came to another alley, approached it warily, his Colt lifted. A dry twig crackled under his right boot. He dropped to one knee, expecting a shot. None came. The darkness here was thick and oppressive.

He cut into the alley, walked softly back toward th main street. Nothing stirred in the deep shadows. But steady warning quivered in the still air. The silence wa solid, yet volatile.

At the mouth of the alley he paused to study the stree At this end of town all the buildings were in darkness There was a vagrant shout from the direction of the hotel The crowd was waiting now, sensing the nature of thi grim fight and the way in which it would have to b resolved.

Frazer's narrowed eyes darted from building to build ing, prying into the shadows. Suddenly a hot wave o feeling poured through him. Almost directly opposite hin at the head of a facing alley there was a vague, indefin able stir in the shadows. It was nothing more than a meager leavening of the deep darkness. Frazer made his guess that Winston was stationed there. Even now Winston probably was watching the alley out of which Frazer must come.

Frazer was reasonably certain Winston could not see him since he was flattened against the wall of the building on his right. Now, with a sudden eager light glinting in his eyes, Frazer retreated toward the rear lots. Once out of the alley, he ran lightly but swiftly along the trash-littered ground that jutted beyond the town's scattered stores. He traveled an entire block before racing up another alley to the main street. Here, too, the street was in darkness.

Winston would be watching the buildings directly in his line of vision. He would not be looking for his quarry this far south. Accordingly, Frazer crouched low and dashed across the street into another narrow aperture between stores.

Reaching the empty back lots west of town, he cut back toward Winston's position. He was careful to count the number of stores he passed. Then, at last, he came to

218

he alley at the head of which the Circle W rancher was osted.

Frazer drifted into the opening, started a slow glide oward the street. He moved with a catlike stealth. His un was held hip high. Excitement tugged at his nerves. But when the showdown arrived he knew he'd be cool.

He got within thirty yards of Winston and still Winston lid not turn. The Circle W rancher was half-flatted against the wall of the building on his left, but he faced he main street.

Frazer pulled to the center of the alley and stopped. His low, flat voice reached out for Winston like a plucking hand.

"Look behind you, Winston!"

Winston whirled and shot in one frenzied motion. It was what Frazer had expected him to do. The bullet slammed into the wall of the building close to Frazer's right arm. Then Frazer's gun roared into the echo of Winston's Colt. The big rancher uttered a stifled gasp, reeled against the building wall, and slid down it to the ground. Frazer heard the dull clatter of his gun striking the earth. He ran forward, dropped beside Winston, and placed the palm of his hand against his chest. His heart was still. Winston was dead.

Frazer rose slowly and walked out into the street. Light in the form of a waving lantern moved toward him from the north end of town. He hurried forward, striding to meet the knot of men advancing from the hotel. Then a slender figure, topped by curly hair, broke from that group and ran out ahead.

"Tom!" It was Margo.

"It's all right, Margo," Frazer called.

He heard her cry something unintelligible. Then she was running forward. She reached him and flung herself into his arms.

219

"Oh, Tom!" she sobbed. "I—I was afraid for you. She lifted her face. "The sheriff said he thought it wa Van Winston. Was it?"

Frazer nodded, still holding her close and liking th feel of her warm body against his. Having Margo in thi manner was all that he asked out of life.

"It's all over, Margo," he murmured. "The fight i won." Then he looked down at her, his eyes intent o hers. His need of her was never so great as at this mo ment. It was a stark hunger staring out of his eyes. H said roughly, "But for us, Margo, this is only the begin ning. Right?"

Margo's arms slid along his chest and up around hi neck. The warm magic of love glowed in her eyes. He mouth was a warm red curve tilted toward him. "Yes Tom," she whispered. "Only the beginning."

He kissed her then. And the passion that burned in him awakened a swift response in Margo. She clung to him as if she couldn't bear to let him go again.

Suddenly they became aware of voices around them. Margo drew out of Frazer's arms. Landon, a makeshift bandage lashed to his side, came up at the head of the crowd. Someone flashed a lantern.

"Winston?" the sheriff inquired.

"Yeah," said Frazer. "Van played out his hand and lost." Frazer pointed to the alley a few yards beyond him. "He's lying back there."

Landon nodded. "He can lie there awhile yet. The crowd here has heard the real story. Some of the boys are ready to ride for the hills to see about rounding up those cattle. As for Ella, Doc Marlow says she'll be all right. She's got a couple of smashed ribs and a concussion."

With his arm still around Margo, Frazer lifted his red head and said, "Glad to hear Ella will pull through." He

220

grinned and some of the ingrained hardness went out of his features. "The cattle can wait until morning."

Landon stared at Frazer, then at Margo. She blushed in the flickering light of the lantern. But she let her head remain in the angle of Frazer's shoulder.

"I reckon they can," Landon agreed, and matched Frazer's grin with a grin of his own.

All Time Bestsellers

- ☐ THE AELIAN FRAGMENT—
  George Bartram   08587-8   1.95
- ☐ THE BERLIN CONNECTION—
  Johannes Mario Simmel   08607-6   1.95
- ☐ THE BEST PEOPLE—Helen Van Slyke   08456-1   1.75
- ☐ A BRIDGE TOO FAR—Cornelius Ryan   08373-5   1.95
- ☐ THE CAESAR CODE—
  Johannes M. Simmel   08413-8   1.95
- ☐ THE CAIN CONSPIRACY—
  Johannes Mario Simmel   08535-5   1.95
- ☐ DO BLACK PATENT LEATHER SHOES
  REALLY REFLECT UP?—John R. Powers   08490-1   1.75
- ☐ THE HAB THEORY—Allen W. Eckerty   08597-5   2.50
- ☐ THE HEART LISTENS—Helen Van Slyke   08520-7   1.95
- ☐ TO KILL A MOCKINGBIRD—Harper Lee   08376-X   1.50
- ☐ THE LAST BATTLE—Cornelius Ryan   08381-6   1.95
- ☐ THE LAST CATHOLIC IN AMERICA—
  J. R. Powers   08528-2   1.50
- ☐ THE LONGEST DAY—Cornelius Ryan   08380-8   1.75
- ☐ THE MIXED BLESSING—Helen Van Slyke   08491-X   1.95
- ☐ THE MONTE CRISTO COVER UP
  Johannes Mario Simmel   08563-0   1.95
- ☐ MORWENNA—Anne Goring   08604-1   1.95
- ☐ THE RICH AND THE RIGHTEOUS
  Helen Van Slyke   08585-1   1.95
- ☐ WEBSTER'S NEW WORLD
  DICTIONARY OF THE AMERICAN
  LANGUAGE   08500-2   1.75
- ☐ WEBSTER'S NEW WORLD THESAURUS   08385-9   1.50
- ☐ THE WORLD BOOK OF HOUSE
  PLANTS—E. McDonald   03152-2   1.50

Buy them at your local bookstores or use this handy coupon for ordering:

Popular Library, P.O. Box 5755, Terre Haute, Indiana 47805   B-5

Please send me the books I have checked above. Orders for less than 5 books must include 60c for the first book and 25c for each additional book to cover mailing and handling. Orders of 5 or more books postage is Free. I enclose $_____ in check or money order.

Name_____

Address_____

City_____ State/Zip_____

Please allow 4 to 5 weeks for delivery. This offer expires 6/78.